Horace Walpole, Francis Blackburne

A Critical Commentary on Archbishop Secker's Letter

to the Right Honourable Horatio Walpole, concerning bishops in America

Horace Walpole, Francis Blackburne

A Critical Commentary on Archbishop Secker's Letter
to the Right Honourable Horatio Walpole, concerning bishops in America

ISBN/EAN: 9783337196332

Printed in Europe, USA, Canada, Australia, Japan

Cover: Foto ©Andreas Hilbeck / pixelio.de

More available books at **www.hansebooks.com**

A CRITICAL
COMMENTARY
ON
Archbiſhop SECKER's Letter
TO THE
Right Honourable HORATIO WALPOLE,
CONCERNING
BISHOPS in AMERICA.

——— *Meditor eſſe affabilis,*
Et bene procedit.——— ———
Paulatim plebem primulùm facio meam.

LONDON:

Printed for E. and C. DILLY, in the Poultry.

M DCC LXX.

A CRITICAL

COMMENTARY, &c.

BEFORE we examine the contents of this remarkable Letter to Mr *Walpole*, it will be neceffary to confider fome circumftances relative to the occafion on which it was written, the time when, and the reafon why it was publifhed.

Archbifhop *Secker*, being himfelf a very fincere convert from the religious errors in which he had been educated in the early part of his life, and zealoufly attached to that fyftem which he afterwards embraced, appears, by many tokens, to have been folicitous to convince thofe whom he had left, of their dangerous ·delufions, and to bring as many of them as he could influence, over to the Church in which he himfelf had found fo much fatisfaction.

With thefe fentiments, and in this attachment to them, it is not at all furprifing, that his Grace fhould be deeply enamoured of this project of

eftablifhing

eſtabliſhing Biſhops in our *American* Colonies.
By ſome intimations in his ſermon preached before *The Society for the Propagation of the Goſpel
in foreign Parts*, February 20, 174$\frac{9}{1}$, it appears,
that the accompliſhment of it had early taken
poſſeſſion of his Grace's affections; and from the
tenor of his conduct and converſation from that
time to the hour of his death, we may ſafely conclude, Mr *Walpole*'s Letter muſt have been a
precious morſel to him, as it gave him an opportunity of figuring on his favourite ſubject before
a miniſter of ſtate.

Mr *Walpole*'s Letter, we are informed by an
Advertiſement prefixed to the Biſhop's, was written in the year 1750, to the late Dr *Sherlock* then
Biſhop of *London*. It does not appear that Biſhop
Sherlock gave any anſwer to it, either by word or
writing. Biſhop *Secker* indeed *ſuppoſes*, " that if
" my Lord of *London* had ever converſed with
" Mr *Walpole* on the ſubject, ſince he received
" Mr *Walpole*'s Letter, he had *doubtleſs* ſaid every
" thing material by way of reply ;" yet nothing
of this ſort appears, and as nothing in writing by
way of anſwer from Dr *Sherlock* to Mr *Walpole*
was known to Dr *Secker**, the more probable
ſuppoſition is, that Biſhop *Sherlock*, convinced by
Mr *Walpole*'s Letter of the danger, the folly, or
at leaſt of the inexpedience of the project, made
no reply at all.

But

* See his Letter, p. 1.

But the moment it is communicated to Dr
Secker, he eagerly feizes the opportunity, and attempts to anfwer the Statesman's objections; very
little, one would think, to that Gentleman's fatisfaction, who from the beginning of the year
1751, to the day of his death, feems to have let
this Letter lie quietly by him, as other fchemes
might do with other minifters of ftate, who
fhould be in no difpofition to be amufed with
the vifionary propofals of weak or defigning projectors.

But fince his Grace's executors, in compliance
with his *fiat* of *May* 25, 1759, have thought fit
to revive this Letter, may we not afk, What is
become of Mr *Walpole*'s Letter to Bifhop *Sherlock?*
That Dr *Secker*, and confequently his executors,
had it in their power to publifh Mr *Walpole*'s
Letter, is very probable. If any circumftances
made it either impracticable or improper to publifh that Letter, candor and common juftice required, that this anfwer to it fhould have been
fuppreffed for the fame length of time. If the
public had any claim upon Archbifhop *Secker* for
his fentiments concerning *American* Bifhops, they
had likewife a right to the whole procefs which
drew thofe fentiments from him. Mr *Walpole*'s
Letter might have objections in it, which Archbifhop *Secker* did not think proper to touch, and
his Grace could not be uninformed, that to publifh anfwers to treatifes, which they who fhould

judge

judge between the parties have no poffible means of confulting, has always been a ftanding and a very reafonable prejudice againft the fairnefs and impartiality of the anfwerers.

As Mr *Walpole*'s Letter is thus withheld, we can only conjecture, that it might be occafioned by fome previous converfation between himfelf and the Bifhop of *London*, concerning Bifhops in *America*. It is very unlikely Mr *Walpole* fhould begin the fubject. Minifters of ftate were *then* faid to be particularly cautious of giving offence to the Colonifts, and thefe, they could not but know, had no predilection for Epifcopacy. The Colonifts, on the other hand, who were members of the Church of *England*, were more efpecially within the Bifhop of *London*'s epifcopal depart-ment. It was therefore natural enough for his Lordfhip to propofe an improvement of *their* re-ligious condition. It was his peculiar bufinefs to remove, as far as he could, all obftacles to it, and confequently to anfwer Mr *Walpole*'s Letter. He did not anfwer it. He plainly thought it un-neceffary.

How then came this province to be turned over to the Bifhop of *Oxford?* If we look no far-ther than the *Advertifement* before the Pamphlet, there is fome appearance of a reafon for it. We are there informed, that Mr *Walpole*'s Letter was communicated to Bifhop *Secker*, by the Bifhop of *London*. And hence it might feem, that the
Bifhop

Bishop of *London*, having either lefs leifure, or lefs ability, left Mr *Walpole* in the hands of his brother of *Oxford*. But in the very firft page of this anfwer, Bifhop *Secker* fays, Mr *Walpole*'s Letter was communicated to him by Mr *Walpole* himfelf; nor does he feem to know any thing at all of the Bifhop of *London*'s fentiments on the fubject of that Letter. It may therefore be fur-mifed, that Bifhop *Secker* was fet to work merely by his own alacrity in fo good a caufe.

There is little doubt but the editors of this Letter think themfelves well juftified in execut-ing his Grace's order for printing it after his death, as well as in taking an early opportunity to do it. And yet, might they not have had a reafonable apology for demurring to that order at this particular juncture, when any attempt at religious innovations in our Colonies, feems to be highly unfeafonable?

At the 15th page of this Letter, his Grace moves a queftion, " Whether the appointment " of Bifhops in the Colonies, would not ftir up " dangerous *uneafineffes* abroad or at home? "

There is I think little doubt but that thefe un-eafineffes had been reprefented to Bifhop *Sherlock*, by Mr *Walpole* (who had very good opportunities of knowing) as the inevitable confequences of fuch an appointment.

But whatever of this kind might then be appre-hended, Archbifhop *Secker* lived to fee *uneafineffes*

in

in the Colonies of a very different nature from any that were dreamt of eighteen years ago : such indeed as might have suggested to him, that nothing could be more unseasonable, than the trying his favourite experiment at a time when every wise and good man, and every well-wisher to the peace and prosperity of his Majesty's government, saw how necessary it was to avoid all occasions of irritating the British Colonists of *America.* His Grace's arguments, in answer to the question abovementioned, whatever weight they might have in 1751, or even in 1759, are lighter than vanity itself, when applied to the state of things in 1768. And whoever peruses a tenth part of the pamphlets which have appeared, during the late altercations on Colony-subjects, will easily perceive, that the publication of such a Letter as this, in the midst of these jarrings, would be adding fuel to the flame. And yet the written order for the printing of it had laid by his Grace, as appears, from 1759 to the time of his death, without one reflection of the very ill effects it might have when he was gone. And could his executors think of doing any honour to his Grace's prudence, his charity, or his moderation, by exposing to the public his Grace's earnestness for advancing his project, at the hazard of so much confusion as must have attended any attempt to execute it at that time?

Perhaps

Perhaps it may be faid, that as our Colony-difputes did not commence till fome years after 1759, his Grace, through the importance and multiplicity of other affairs, might forget he had made an order for printing this piece after his death. But this I think will hardly be allowed by thofe who confider, what daily occurred in the news papers, concerning the project of epifco-pizing *America*; or if it might be fuppofed that thefe were below his Grace's notice, the exiftence of fuch an order could not poffibly efcape his memory during his Grace's controverfy with Dr *Mayhew*, in which fome of the fame topics are exhibited on the part of his Grace, that we find in this Letter to Mr *Walpole*. And as the fubject has been kept in public view, more or lefs, to this very time, there cannot be the leaft doubt but the Archbifhop was confcious of this order, as long as he was confcious of any thing.

However, fince this Letter muft be publifhed, it was not unwifely done to poftpone it till after his Grace's deceafe. How aptly foever the contents of it might have come in aid of his Grace's other arguments for *American* Epifcopacy, he faw no doubt the additional imputations it muft have brought him under, from his petulant reflections upon our domeftic Diffenters, not to mention the danger of a more mortifying reproof for throwing a bone of contention when and where the parties concerned were fufficiently exafperated without it.

What

What fhall we fay for his Grace on this occafion? Shall we offer the apology that one of his admirers hath fuggefted for his intermeddling in the expulfion of the *Oxford* Students? *viz.* " A " body labouring under great infirmities, and a " mind perhaps fympathifing with it, and his " not poffeffing in their full vigour thofe great " faculties, for which he was once fo´eminently " diftinguifhed *."

But if this apology for his Grace is accepted, what muft be faid for the editors of the Letter in queftion? Muft not thefe infirmities of body and mind have been more familiarly known to them, than to others who had no particular connections at *Lambeth?* Will his Grace's order fufficiently excufe them to the public for a production of this nature, *born* fo much *out of due time?* It had been fufficient for their fcruples on the peremptorinefs of the order, to have *printed* the Letter, and to have withheld the *publication*, till times more favourable to the caufe it pleads. It is remarkable, that juft before it was advertifed, the public prints gave us notice, that our Colonydifputes were upon the point of being adjufted to the fatisfaction of all parties: and this was the more credible, as it was announced by writers who were underftood to be retained as advocates

for

* Strictures on Dr *Nowel's* Anfwer to *Pietas Oxonienfis*, page 37, 38.

for the adminiſtration *. At this critical juncture, could there be any laudable, any excuſable
motive for publiſhing theſe papers ſo full fraught
with provocation to our Diſſenters at home, as
well as their brethren in the Colonies abroad ?
And will not this inconſiderate deference for his
Grace's commands, juſtify the enemies of the
Church in a common obſervation, that, provided
the dignity and emoluments of the Hierarchy are
but maintained, no matter what becomes of the
civil intereſt of the community; and will not the
editors, as well as the author, come in for their
ſhare of this reproach ?

Paſs we on from theſe preliminary remarks, to
the contents of the Letter.

" The thing propoſed, ſays Dr *Secker*, is, that
" two or three perſons ſhould be ordained Bi-
" ſhops, and ſent into our American Colonies, to
" adminiſter Confirmation, and to give Deacon's
" and Prieſt's orders to proper candidates; and
" exerciſe ſuch juriſdiction over the Clergy of
" the Church of *England*, in thoſe parts, as the
" late Biſhop of *London*'s Commiſſaries did; or
" ſuch as it might be thought proper that any
" future Commiſſaries ſhould, if this deſign were
" not to take place." *page* 2.

By the alternative in the latter part of this propoſal, it ſhould ſeem, that, " if this deſign were
" not

" not to take place," it might be thought proper to veſt the *future* Commiſſaries of the Biſhop
of *London* with larger powers of jurisdiction, than
the late Commiſſaries had enjoyed, in order to
ſupply the want of Epiſcopal jurisdiction. To
what this new jurisdiction of the future Commiſſaries would amount, we are not informed. It
is left indefinite. This we may ſafely conclude,
that it would *not* be thought proper to limit the
jurisdiction of Biſhops to any thing leſs than it
may be thought proper the future Commiſſaries
ſhould exerciſe; and this might, and probably
would be, the full jurisdiction exerciſed by the
Biſhops of the mother country. What effect this
diſcovery will have, upon ſome other propoſals
in this Letter, we ſhall ſee preſently. In the mean
time we proceed with the writer of it.

" The queſtions, ſaith Dr *Secker*, which ariſe
" on this propoſal, are, Is it a reaſonable pro-
" poſal in itſelf? And if it be, are there any
" ſuch dangers of its being extended to intro-
" duce exorbitant church powers, or of raiſing
" uneaſineſſes abroad or at home, as may not-
" withſtanding, at leaſt for the preſent, be juſt
" objections againſt it (*a*) ? "

His Grace ſets out with inſinuating, that,
" Mr *Walpole* ſeemed to allow the reaſonableneſs
" of the propoſal, abſtractedly conſidered." But
as this only *ſeems* to have been the caſe, we cannot

(*a*) Page 2.

not judge under what abftraction Mr *Walpole* allowed the reafonablenefs of the propofal. This could only be learned from his Letter, to which we have no accefs.

Dr *Secker* argues for the reafonablenefs of the propofal from what belongs to the very nature of Epifcopal Churches; and concerning this matter, Mr *Walpole* might very widely differ from the Dr. —— Mr *Walpole* might be of opinion, that many things belong to the nature of Epifcopal Churches, which the Bifhops of *England* do not bring into practice. He might afk the Bifhop of *London*, Whether the Bifhops of *England* enjoyed any privileges, or exercifed any jurisdiction, which do *not* belong to the very nature of Epifcopal Churches? If yea: it feems expedient to retrench thefe in the firft place, as mere ufurpations, feeing that no edification can arife from the exercife of fuch powers and privileges. If, on the other hand, the *Englifh* Bifhops exercife no jurisdiction which does not belong to the nature of Epifcopal Churches; and if it is reafonable to fend Bifhops to *America*, it muft be reafonable to fend them with the powers and privileges which belong to the very nature of the Churches over which they are intended to prefide. That is to fay, with the powers and privileges exercifed and enjoyed by the Bifhops of *England*. But this Dr *Secker* did *not defire* we fhould believe. Why was he not then more

explicit

explicit concerning the jurisdiction it might be thought proper the new Bishops should exercise in *America* ?

" It belongs, says Dr *Secker*, to the very na-
" ture of Episcopal Churches to have Bishops,
" at proper distances, presiding over them (*b*)."
Not only that, but it belongs to the nature of Episcopal Churches to have Bishops at *certain* distances, that is to say, within certain districts called Dioceses, presiding over them, and consequently residing among them. For it must be remembered, that there are certain things belonging to the nature of the Episcopal *Office*, as well as to the nature of Episcopal *Churches*, one of which is *vigilance* over the flock of which the Bishop takes the charge; which cannot be exercised while he is absent from them, either in *England* or *America*: and this is equally true, whether the Bishop is distant some hundreds, or some thousands of miles from his Diocese. And yet we know the inhabitants of some of our Dioceses, are, in this respect, no better accommodated than the inhabitants of *America*, for three parts of the year out of four.

If it should be said, *English* Bishops can perform the necessary acts of vigilance by their officers stationed in the Diocese; even so may the Bishop of *London* by his Commissaries stationed in *America*.

" But,

(*b*) Page 3.

" But, it is alledged, that there are Epifcopal
" Acts, which muft be performed by Bifhops in
" perfon," and of thefe the firft inftance is that
of *Confirmation*.

Shall we then lay it down for a rule, that it
belongs to the nature of Epifcopal Churches,
that all their members fhould be *Confirmed ?* If
it does not, the Colonifts may do without it.
And that it does not, appears from the practice,
and indeed from the conftitution of the Church
of *England*. In feveral Diocefes there are no
Confirmations for feveral years. When Confirmation is adminiftered, it is to children or young
perfons, from the age of thirteen to fixteen in-
clufive.

By Canon CXII. if perfons of the age of fixteen do not communicate, they are to be pre-
fented to the Archbifhop, by the Minifter,
Churchwardens, &c. In confequence of this
Canon, thoufands receive the Communion who
were never Confirmed, becaufe they never had
an opportunity. And when fuch communicants
prefent themfelves for Confirmation, they are
told, it is not proper, after they have communicated; which fhews, that how *ufeful* foever Confirmation may be, where it *can* be had, where it
cannot, it is, by the conftitution of the Church
of *England* herfelf, *unneceffary*. And after this,
would it be fufficiently refpectful to my Lords
the Bifhops, or indeed to our *excellent* eftablifhment

ment to fay, that fuch and fuch people, of *Cumber-
land* for inftance, or *Northumberland*, or the *Welch*
Counties, are denied Confirmation, unlefs they
will go to *London* for it ? or that they are in effect
prohibited the exercife of one part of their religion (*c*) ?

With refpect to Ordination, there are two ex-
pedients in ufe at prefent for furnifhing the Colonifts of the Church of *England* with Minifters of
their own Communion; 1. By ordaining natives
of *America* who come to *England* for that purpofe.
2. By fending *Englifh* Minifters to the Colonies
from hence.

As to the firft of thefe, Dr *Secker* obferves, that
" fending their fons to fo diftant a climate muft
" be very inconvenient and difagreeable, and tak-
" ing the fmall-pox here is faid to be peculiarly
" fatal to them," *i. e.* peculiarly to the perfons
who come here for Orders. For when his Grace
mentions a little below, that, " their young men
" of fafhion would ftill come to *England* for polite
" accomplifhments," no apprehenfions of what
would be inconvenient or difagreeable to *them*,
are expreffed, nor any mention made of any *peculiar* fatality of the fmall-pox to fuch young men.

" The expence alfo, fays his Grace, muft be
" grievous to perfons of fmall fortunes, fuch as
" moft are who breed up their children for Or-
" ders; and yet not fufficient to bring any accef-
" fion

" fion of wealth to this Nation that would be
" worth naming, were more of that rank to
" come." (d)

From the caft of this anfwer, one may conjecture, that Mr *Walpole* had objected to *American*
Bifhops, that fuch a meafure would prevent the
Colonifts from coming hither, and fpending their
money among us. To obviate this, his Grace
was obliged to fuppofe, that none would fend their
Sons to *England* to be ordained, but perfons in
mean circumftances. But I am inclined to believe
that the Statesman's objection would ftrike a little
deeper, and that the confideration with him might
be, that the more inducements the Colonifts in general fhould have to ftay at home, and the fewer
occafions of perfonal intercourfe with the mother
country, the more they would afpire to indepen-
dency; a matter of very ferious Confideration
among the Minifters of thofe times *.

The Statesman, no doubt, argued, that if the
Colonifts of the Church of *England* were impow-

B ered

(d) Letter, page 4.

* I have been informed, that the late Archbifhop *Secker*,
being in conference with an eminent Colonift, defired to know
of him, if his countrymen would be averfe to the fending a
Bifhop among them ? *Pray, my Lord*, faid the Gentleman,
can one Bifhop make another ? Undoubtedly, *replied* his Grace.
Why then, my Lord, rejoined the Colonift, *you may fend your
Bifhop as foon as you pleafe, it will be one confiderable ftep towards our living without you.* Here the converfation was
dropped.

ered to manufacture Deacons and Priests for themfelves, as well as other things, which they have hitherto imported from hence, they would in time
have a Church independent upon that in the mother
country ; a confideration of ten times more importance to Mr *Walpole*, than the money that would
be gained by a few young Men coming to *England*
for Orders, or that would be loft by their ftaying
away.

2. With refpect to the Clergymen of the Church
of *England* who are fent from hence, it muft be
a matter of great Concern to all who wifh well to
the interefts and credit of the eftablifhment, to be
told by an Archbifhop of *Canterbury*, that few of
them, in proportion, " can anfwer the end for
" which they are defigned (e)." That the reft are
" men of defperate fortunes, low qualifications,
" bad and doubtful characters, and a great part
" of them *Scotch* Jacobites." Is this for the honour of the Society which fends them ? How
greatly does this reprefentation detract from the
credibility of thofe accounts they give us from
time to time, of the fuccefs of their labours in our
Plantations ; which depend, in a great meafure,
on the veracity of men of thefe wretched Characters ? When the public is folicited, as is often the
cafe, to fupply the deficiency of the Society's funds,
by their charitable contributions, will they not
be

(e) Page 4.

be apt to confider, before they give their money, upon what fort of Men it is to be expended?

And how would the matter be mended by fending Bifhops inftead of Priefts? Every confideration drawn from the nature of the fervice, the danger of the voyage, abfence from family-connexions, &c. which at prefent ferves to difcourage private Clergymen of eafy fortunes, good learning, found principles, and refpectable characters, would operate with equal force upon the mind of a deftined Bifhop, and create the fame reluctance that other men have fhewn to engage in fuch an adventure.

We his Grace have faid in anfwer to this, that a larger ftipend, an increafe of power, and a more refpectable title, would have engaged more reputable candidates? I am afraid this would be only faying, that ambition and avarice are more reputable motives for accepting the office of a chriftian Bifhop, than the profpect of a bare maintenance is for taking the province of an ordinary teacher. His Grace could hardly think that the Colonifts are fo much ftrangers to human nature, as not to be aware, that thefe difpofitions are common to Clergymen and others, both of higher and lower ranks; and that, with refpect to Bifhops fent from *England* to *America*, the fame hazards muft be run by the fenders, to which the propagating Society is liable in difpatching common Miffionaries. So that all the good things his Grace augurates from the appointment of Colony-Bifhops

would

would effectually be fruſtrated, if the Biſhops were no better men (a point his Grace could by no means inſure to the Coloniſts) than the Miſſionaries he ſpeaks of.

His Grace propoſes great benefit, and conſiderable reformation among both the conforming Clergy and Laity in our Colonies, by ſubſtituting natives for their ordinary Paſtors, inſtead of *vagabond ſtrangers*, (as he calls the Miſſionaries ſent from *England*.) But if native Miniſters would ſo much improve the religious ſtate of our Church-of-*England* Coloniſts, why not native Biſhops? I aſk this queſtion, becauſe it appears to me, that his Grace never dreamt of ſupplying the mortality of Colony Biſhops, otherwiſe than by recruits from *England.* Probably his grand point could not be gained any other way. Otherwiſe a native of ſome of the Colonies, not liable to the fatality of the ſmall-pox, or to much inconvenience of another ſort, might come over and be conſecrated once for all in *England.* Or an *Engliſh* or an *Iriſh* Biſhop might be found without much difficulty, who would undertake the voyage, without the mortifying alternative of bidding a final adieu to his European connexions, and, having conſecrated one or more proper perſons from among the natives, might return home, and leave the Coloniſts to improve their religious ſtate upon this new inſtitution, as they found occaſion. Here indeed would be *additional encouragement* to parents to breed their children to the Church, — ftill more *convenient opportu-nities* of providing for them handfomely, and even to build and endow, not only Churches and parfonage houfes, but Cathedrals and Bifhops palaces, in which good works they would hardly fhew fo much alacrity, if they found the honour, emolument, and power appropriated to Bifhops fent in fucceffion from *England*.

And what, I defire to know, would hinder a Bifhop fent from *England* from appearing to the Colonifts in the light of a *vagabond ftranger*, any more than a common Miffionary? And would he be more likely, with this *ftigma* upon him, to anfwer any of 'the good ends propofed by his Grace, more effectually than any other Clergyman of the fame country? And this being the cafe, all that is propofed by his Grace in fending Bifhops from hence, is a mere empty chimerical vifion, which deferves not the leaft regard.

Mr *Walpole* muft have been a weak politician indeed, if he did not fee that Bifhops fent from *England* would increafe the evils complained of, rather than remedy them. He muft have been fenfible, or if he was not, we may be at this hour, that the Colonifts, were they inclined to admit a pre-latical Hierarchy among them (which he very well knew none of them were) would never be fatis-fied without having the whole ordering of it themfelves, any more than they chufe to be con-troled in fome other things. And leaft of all

would

would they submit to be governed by *English*
Bishops.

One of the blessed effects of the reformation
proposed by his Grace (in my opinion the principal one in his estimation) was the conversion of
the Dissenters. Accordingly, he strains every
nerve to magnify the advantages of this event
to the public, in a political view.

" If, saith his Grace, by reforming them (the
" Colonists of the Church of *England*) and in-
" troducing better order into the Churches of
" our communion, more of the inhabitants should
" come over to it, *as they naturally will*, this
" would be a further public benefit. For the
" members of the Church of *England* will think
" themselves more connected with *England*, than
" others *."

Have then the non-conforming Colonists no
dissenting brethren, no kindred, no commercial
interests, no King in *England?* Have they less
connection, or fewer attachments to *England*, on
these and other accounts, than the conformists
themselves ?

* Page 5. I have good grounds for affirming, that the
Conformists in the Colonies in general, so far from being
more inclined to keep up their connections with the mother
country, never did so much by a thousand times, for the sake
of it, as the Dissenters ever did, before, and for years after
this Letter was written. This however is not meant to exclude some particular public-spirited Conformists. Who they
were, and of what communion, who were chiefly instru-
mental in the late misunderstandings between the Colonies
and the mother country, I have no inclination to inquire.

themfelves? If this had been infinuated by a lefs venerable character than that of an Archbifhop, I fhould have been tempted to fay, that the man muft either be contemptible for his ignorance, or of an abandoned affurance, who fhould venture fuch a fuggeftion among thofe who know the truth of the cafe.

His Grace goes on. " And fuppofing them " not to be *Jacobites*, their acknowledgment of " the King's fupremacy, will incline them to be " dutifuller fubjects than the Diffenters, who do " do not acknowledge it." (g)

Suppofing them not to be Jacobites! whom does he mean? plainly the converts from among the Diffenters. But whoever accufed the Non conformifts in the Colonies of *Jacobitifm*, even any one man among them? There is therefore not the leaft colour for this fuppofition, unlefs we fuppofe that thefe converts become *Jacobites* as foon as they become Conformifts; which is no very defirable effect of the Epifcopal reformation here held forth.

On another hand, his Grace has more than fuppofed that moft of the *Scotch* miffionaries are *Jacobites*. But every one knows that all thefe, to be duly qualified for their office, muft acknowledge the King's fupremacy upon oath: a plain proof that the greater or lefs dutifulnefs of

B 4   the

(g) Page 6.

the fubject does not depend upon fuch acknowledgment.

But, " the Diffenters do not acknowledge the
" King's fupremacy." I am confident that this
is a mere malevolent mifreprefentation, and that
there is not one Diffenter in the Colonies, who
denies the King to be his fupreme Governor ;
and I am perfuaded the fame may be faid for
every proteftant Diffenter in *Great Britain*.

The true cafe is this. The proteftant Diffenters hold, that the civil magiftrate hath no authority to interfere in matters of religion, which
do not affect the fafety of his government, fo
far as the private judgment or confcience of his
fubjects is concerned, whether confidered as in-
dividuals, or united in religious fociety : and this
they hold, not merely with refpect to the authority of a King or a Monarch as fuch, but of the
aggregate power of legiflature however confti-
tuted. And is this principle peculiar to Diffenters ? Has it not been, is it not ftill the principle of as wife, learned, and worthy Conformifts
as ever exifted ? Was it not the principle of
Locke, Burnet, Clark, Hoadley, and others of the
laft generation ? And had the Kings or Queens
of thofe times when thefe men flourifhed, *dutifuller* fubjects (to ufe his Grace's elegant language) than thefe illuftrious perfons, in the king-
dom ? Does not the artificial author of the *Alli-
ance in Church and State*, inform us, that this was
the

the principle on which the Toleration Act was grounded ? And would his Grace himſelf have ventured to ſay, had he been catechiſed on this head, that it was *not* his own principle too ?

I aſk his pardon, I did not think of a paſſage in this Letter, *page* 13. where his Grace believes, " his Majeſty hath not a right to order the " Biſhop of *London* to recall his Commiſſaries." And if ſo, the ſupremacy, according to his Grace's creed, muſt, in this inſtance, be in the Biſhop of *London*, and not in the King.

For the reſt, if it was ever underſtood that the proteſtant Diſſenters denied the King's ſupremacy, as oppoſed to the ſupremacy of the Pope, or of any foreign Potentate, it is more than I ever heard. In the mean time, it is well known, that the Diſſenters ſcruple not to put themſelves under the protection of the law, as their *dernier reſort*, whenever they apprehend their rights, even as a religious ſociety, to be infringed, or attempted, as was lately notorious in the caſe of a Diſſenter named to the office of Sheriff of *London*, which received its deciſion in the *ſupreme* court of judicature of *Great Britain*.

2. We are now come to the ſecond queſtion, namely, " Whether the danger of increaſing " Church power, by the means of eſtabliſhing " Biſhops in *America*, is not a ſufficient objection " againſt the project ?"

In

In the outſet of his Letter, his Grace talks of " juriſdiction over the Clergy, not only ſuch as " the late Biſhop of *London's* Commiſſaries *did* " exerciſe, but ſuch as it might be thought " proper future Commiſſaries *ſhould* exerciſe, if " this deſign of epiſcopiſing, ſhould not take " place." An inſinuation that is utterly incon-ſiſtent with his Grace's declaration, that, " *con-* " *firming* and *ordaining* are the only *new* powers " that *will* be exerciſed (*b*)." Theſe powers of confirming and ordaining, the Commiſſaries never had ; nor, tenacious as our Prelates have always been of reſerving theſe powers to themſelves, is it probable they will ever cónſent that future Commiſſaries ſhould be inveſted with them. The juriſdiction, therefore, that it may be thought proper theſe future Commiſſaries *ſhould* exerciſe, muſt ſignify that enlargement of Church power on which the objection is founded. And as this *enlargement* is intended as a *ſuccedaneum*, in the room of Epiſcopal power, few people will be per-ſuaded it will be leſs obnoxious in the hands of Biſhops, than it would be in the hands of Com-miſſaries.

His Grace, therefore, may much more ſafely be believed, when he ſays, that, " ſtrictly ſpeak-" ing, it can never be promiſed, *in any caſe*, that " no additional powers ſhall hereafter be propoſed " and preſſed on the Colonies," than when he

ſays,

(*b*) Page 6.

fays, " no other jurisdiction is *defired* for the
" propofed Bifhops, than the preceding Com-
" miffaries have enjoyed."

And yet I know not whether we may not fafely
take his Grace's word, even for this laft particular. *Right* and *Title*, are very different things
from actual *enjoyment* ; and if the Colonifts may
be believed, thefe fame Commiffaries have both
enjoyed and exercifed pretended powers of jurifdiction, highly injurious and oppreffive to the
inhabitants, without any *apparent* authority for
it.

And of this his Grace feems to have been confcious; elfe why fhould his Grace have added,
" and even that" [the jurisdiction enjoyed by
former Commiffaries] " on this occafion, may
" be afcertained and limited, *more accurately*, *if*
" *it be requifite (i)*." But will it ever be *thought*
requifite, by thofe who think as his Grace did,
that the jurisdiction of a Bifhop fhould be *afcertained* or *limited* to any mark below that at which
the jurisdiction of a Commiffary hath been *enjoyed?* And indeed, does not this gracious conceffion feem to imply that the jurisdiction which
thefe Commiffaries have enjoyed, was in fact,
unafcertained and *unlimited?*

His Grace fuppofes, " it would have been equally right to have oppofed the Toleration Act, on the
apprehenfion, that more, in confequence of this
                                    conceffion,

(i) Page 6.

conceffion, might have been preffed upon the government in favour of the Diffenters, as to oppofe the fettlement of Bifhops in *America*, from
a prefumption of increafing the power of the
Church (*k*)."

But, I conceive, the cafes are widely different.
Whatever is preffed upon government in favour of the Diffenters, will always be fubject to
the control of Parliament. Whereas his Grace
tells us, *page* 21. " There feems no neceffity that
" this affair" [of eftablifhing American Bifhops]
" fhould ever come into Parliament." The Bifhops, according to his Grace, " would be ap-
" pointed by the Crown, and will be fuch perfons
" as the Crown can beft confide in." *page* 13.
This looks as if the Crown was to have an intereft in thefe Bifhops, diftinct from the intereft
of the public ; and fhould it appear in procefs of
time that the limited powers with which thefe
Bifhops fhould be fent out at the firft, would be
infufficient for the *political* purpofes of the Crown,
can it be doubted but that they would be immediately enlarged ? And can any man fuppofe that
pretences for it would not be furnifhed by our
Bifhops (the only folicitors of the project that the
Letter points out) *viz.* " that it would be a dif-
paragement of the Order, to have Bifhops in
any part of his Majefty's dominions, vefted
with lefs power than the Bifhops of the mother
country.

(*k*) Page 7.

country. — That it belonged to the nature of Epifcopal Churches, that their Bifhops fhould have full powers to correct the tranfgreffions as well of the Laity as the Clergy; and that without thefe powers in their Bifhops, the conforming Colonifts would not have the full exercife of their religion;" would not thefe pleas be full as forceable for enlarging thofe powers, as they are now for appointing the Bifhops themfelves ? *Forceable*, I mean to the Crown, whofe particular confidants thefe American Bifhops are to be. And what or who would there be to fay nay to the propofal, the Crown having the *power*, and the Bifhops the *will*, to have it carried into execution.

But had his Grace reflected ever fo little upon what paffed in Parliament before the Toleration Act was obtained for the Diffenters, his Grace might have eafily perceived, that it was the utmoft that could be obtained for them ; and that King *William* never could prevail to have them brought into civil offices, but under the reftrictions of the Teft Act ; and that the very order of men, who would, as the cafe above is ftated by his Grace, have fo much influence towards enlarging the power of American Bifhops, have hitherto had fufficient intereft to prevent any farther favours, particularly, *any thing hurtful to the eftablifhed Church*, from being conferred on the Diffenters.

His Grace however affures us, that no fuch thing is intended as preffing for *additional* powers

to

to *American* Bifhops; and in this affertion he thinks there are no grounds to queftion the *fincerity* of his Grace and his brethren.

But on this head of *fincerity*, I think it was as much as could be reafonably expected of his Grace, to anfwer for himfelf ; for affuredly he could offer no fatisfactory proof that others of his brethren might not intend, what he did not; and about the time when he thus undertook to anfwer for them, it is certain there were Bifhops who were " thought to be peculiarly fond of Church-power," and who when " they were called upon to anfwer for themfelves," gave very little fatisfaction by their *defences*.

His Grace's great argument for this *fincerity* is, the *moderation* of his contemporaries. To which I fhall fay nothing, but that his Grace was probably the moft improper perfon of them all, to offer this confideration on the behalf of his brethren.

What his Grace's *moderation* was, while he was Bifhop of *Oxford*, I leave to be determined, by thofe who were then under his government ; what it was when he came to be the Head of his Order, the following admonition, intended for his brethren in convocation 1761, will fufficiently fhew.

SEMPER ENITENDUM EST ut ANTIQUI REGI-MINIS non modo retineamus formam, SED ET VIM INSTAUREMUS, quatenus vel DIVINO VEL

HUMANO

HUMANO JURE FULCITUR. Atque INTERIM,
MANCA quodammodo et MUTILA erit πολιτεια
noſtra (*l*).

That is to ſay, *We muſt always* STRIVE, *not
only to retain the form, but to* RENEW THE FORCE
of the ANCIENT CHURCH-GOVERNMENT, *ſo far
as it is* PROPPED UP *either by* DIVINE *or* HUMAN
AUTHORITY. *And till that be done, our* POLITY
will be LAME *and* DEFECTIVE.

Now what was this ancient Church-government? Even the model left us by ſome of his
Grace's Predeceſſors and their adherents, who
never wanted *props* for it (if you would take their
interpretations of ſcripture) either from *divine* or
human authority. And the *force* of it conſiſted,
in putting *a two-edged ſword into the hands of*
Church-Governors, *to execute vengeance upon the
heathen, and puniſhments upon the people* *. In
plain Engliſh, power to correct Heretics, Schiſ-
matics, and Diſſenters, with the wholeſome ſe-
verities of whips, pillories, fines and impriſon-
ment.

Without this *force*, it ſeems our preſent eccleſiaſtical Polity is mutilated and lame ; and it is, in
his Grace's opinion, not only *right* to have this
force

(*l*) *Oratio Synodalis*, at the end of his Grace's Charges,
page 360.

* See Pſalm xlix. 6, 7. To ,which Archbiſhop *Laud* prefixed this title. *The Prophet exhorteth to praiſe God for his
love to the Church : and for that power which he hath given to
the Church, to rule the conſciences of men.*

force *renewed*, but abfolutely the duty of the members of the convocation, to *ftrive* to have it renewed.

" Is this the fame man," may fome people fay,
" who feems in his Letter to Mr *Walpole*, to be
" fo well contented with the fhare of power en-
" joyed by the prefent Bifhops, and who would
" have been fatisfied with much lefs, if he had
" lived where much lefs had been allotted to Bi-
" fhops? Is this the man who ftands forth to af-
" fure the public, that he and his Brethren are
" not fo fond of Church Power, as to be aiming
" at that point now, while they folemnly profefs
" they are not (*m*)?"

For my part, I can fee but little room we can make for the virtue of *fincerity* here. In the *Letter* his Grace affures us, with a folemn face and a fmooth tongue, that nothing more is required for thefe *American* Bifhops, than commiffarial jurisdiction, and authority to *confirm* and ordain. In the *oration*, the ancient Church-government is to be contended for at all events ; and without the *force* of it, the Epifcopal Powers muft be lame and mutilated. Muft we not argue thus? this ancient regimen either belongs to the nature of Epifcopal Churches, or it does not. If it does not, his Grace is exhorting the Convocation to ftrive for *fupporting* the *form*, and *reinftating* the *force* of an ancient ufurpation. If it does, the fame pretence which
ferves

(*m*) Page 8, 9.

ferves for a colour to ftation Bifhops in *America*, will ferve for a pretence to claim for them the *form* and *force* of the ancient government, namely, the pretence that it belongs to the nature of Epis-copal Churches. And this, I fhould think, a-mounts to fomething more than a *poffibility*, that an improper ufe may hereafter be attempted to be made of the appointment of Bifhops for *America*. Once more, what fhall we fay for his Grace's *fince-rity* and his *moderation?* thefe two publications are coeval, and by the time and manner of their ap-pearance, fhould feem between them to exhibit his Grace's dying fentiments.

But the *moderation* and *fincerity*, concerning which, in examining his Grace's portions of them, we are left in fo much uncertainty, we may perhaps find in his Grace's coadjutors in this project, with more precifion. It fometimes happens that men not worth fixpence, will offer their bond for great fums, on the behalf of others who are very well able to pay without them.

" Archbifhop *Tenifon*," fays his Grace, " who " was furely no high Churchman, left £1000 to-" wards the Eftablifhment of Bifhops in *Ameri-* " *ca* (*n*)."

His Grace, I am afraid, is a little unlucky in his inftance; I am in fome doubt whether Arch-bifhop *Tenifon*'s fincerity in this bequeft, is altoge-ther confiftent with Archbifhop *Secker*'s in this pamphlet. But let the reader determine.

In

In Archbifhop *Tenifon*'s Will, executed *April*
11th, 1715, five hundred pounds were bequeathed
to the Society for Propagating the Gofpel in foreign
Parts, " for the purchafing one or more perpe-
" tual advowfons, donations, right of patronage
" and prefentation of, in, and to one or more vi-
" carages or rectories, and to prefent thereto from
" time to time, as often as the fame fhall become
" void, one or more of the moft deferving Mif-
" fionaries of the province of *Canterbury*."

But by a codicil, executed *Dec.* 2. 1715, his
Grace revokes and declares this bequeft null and
void, and in the room of it fubftitutes what follows,

" But my prefent Will is, that my executors,
" their adminiftrators or affigns, do well and tru-
" ly pay to the faid Society, within one month,
" or two at the fartheft, after the appointment and
" confecration by lawful authority of two Proteft-
" tant Bifhops, one for the Continent, another for
" the ifles in *North America*, the fum of one thou-
" fand pounds, to be applied in equal portions to
" the fettlement of fuch Bifhops in the fore-men-
" tioned Sees. *Until fuch lawful appointment and*
" *confecrations are compleated, I am very fenfible*
" *(as many of my brethren of that Society alfo are)*
" *that as there has not hitherto been, notwithftand-*
" *ing much importunity and many promifes to the*
" *contrary, fo there never will or can be any regular*
" *Church difcipline in thofe parts, or any confirma-*
" *tions*

" tions or due ordinations, or any setting apart in
" ecclesiastical manner, of any public places for the
" more decent Worship of God, or any timely pre-
" venting or abating of factions and divisions, which
" have been and are at present very rife; no eccle-
" siastically legal discipline or corrections of scanda-
" lous manners, either in the Clergy or Laity, or
" synodical assemblies, as may be a proper means to
" regulate ecclesiastical proceedings. In the mean
" time, *till such appointment and consecration as
" abovesaid is compleated,* my Will is, that my
" executors do not pay the said thousand pounds,
" or any part or portion of it, or any interest for
" the whole or any part of it to the said Society,
" but as they have opportunity, to put out the
" said sum or part of it to interest upon sure pub-
" lic funds, and to apply such interest to the bene-
" fit of such Missionaries, being Englishmen, and
" of the province of *Canterbury,* as they shall
" find upon good information, to have taken true
" pains in the respective places which have been
" committed by the said Society to their care, in
" the said foreign Plantations, and have been by
" unavoidable accidents, sickness or other infir-
" mities of the body, or old age, disabled from
" the performance of their duties in the said places
" or precincts, and forced to return to *England* "
　　Such is the bequest of Archbishop *Tenison,* in
which we may observe a very different plan of
American Episcopacy from that delineated by his

　　　　　　　　successor,

succeſſor, Dr *Secker*, in this Letter.   We have here the whole Hierarchical apparatus of Engliſh Epiſcopacy enumerated in the minuteſt manner. *Regular Church diſcipline.—Conſecration of Churches.—Prevention of factions and diviſions*, (meaning, I ſuppoſe, proviſions for uniformity)—*Due Ordinations* (which the Coloniſts are ſuppoſed to want, for it ſeems till a Biſhop is appointed there *never will be* any ſuch)—*ecclesiastically-legal corrections both of the Clergy and Laity*.   And to crown all, *Synodical aſſemblies to regulate ecclesiaſtical proceedings.*

From the tenor of this codicil, and particularly from the words, *in the mean time, till ſuch appointment and conſecration as aboveſaid is compleated*, it is clear, that till this ſyſtem of Prelatical jurisdiction is *ſettled* in *North America*, both on the continent and in the iſles, the executors of Archbiſhop *Teniſon*, their adminiſtrators, or aſſigns, will not be obliged to pay a ſingle ſixpence of the thouſand pounds to the propagating Society ; for that ſettlement is plainly *the conſideration* for which the legacy is left : conſequently, it cannot be applied to the maintenance of Biſhops with the limited, and no more than commiſſarial juriſdiction, for which Dr *Secker* pleads.

It cannot in the leaſt be doubted, but his late Grace of *Canterbury* was well acquainted with the contents of this codicil, ſo far as it related to the appointment of *American* Biſhops.   Why then
did

did he content him felf with this general mention of the legacy, and fupprefs the conditions of it? Plainly for too very obvious reafons.

1. Left Mr *Walpole* fhould fufpect his Lord-fhip's *fincerity* in affecting to *defire* no more power for *American* Bifhops, than he feems to plead for in this Letter. Mr *Walpole* would be certain that Dr *Secker*, in cafe he carried his point for *American* Bifhops, would not confent to give up this Legacy of Archbifhop *Tenifon*; and he would naturally conclude, that upon the event of ap-pointing fuch Bifhops, Dr *Secker*, as a man of fenfe, and a man of politics, would make the pre-fervation of the legacy, an argument for granting the additional jurifdiction defcribed in the codicil.

2. The particulars enumerated in the codicil, are utterly inconfiftent with the character of *no high Church-man*, for which he would recommend the example of Archbifhop *Tenifon*. The exhibi-tion of them would indeed have made a farther difcovery, equally unfavourable to the views and principles of *many of* Dr Tenifon's *brethren of the Society*, who are reprefented as equally *fenfible* with his Grace, that all thefe Ecclefiaftical *neceffaries* would follow the appointment of Bifhops, and could not be had without it; and confequently would quite fpoil Dr *Secker*'s argument drawn from the " univerfal defire of his brethren, and of the " members of the Society, as well Laymen as " Clergymen, of eftablifhing Colony Bifhops,

" *from*

" *from the Revolution to this day* ;" and induce a
suspicion that the converson of the Indians was
but a blind, a mere pretence of the high churchmen, to obtain a charter for the nobler purpose of
establishing Bishops.   For his Grace expresly tells
us, that, " this whole body of men, almost ever
" since it was in being, hath been making re-
" peated applications for Bishops in *America* (o)."
Behold then the cloven foot which his Grace, no
doubt, thought was sufficiently covered by this
general reference to Archbishop *Tenison*'s legacy,
as he might be pretty sure Mr *Walpole* would hardly
go to the Commons to consult the original.

I am however persuaded, that there have been,
and still are numbers of that respectable Society,
who fall not under his Grace's crude represfentation.
I could, if it was proper, point out some most worthy men, whose names were not long ago upon
the list, who thought no better of the episcopizing
project than Mr *Walpole*, and particularly as de-
scribed in Archbishop *Tenison*'s codicil.   But the
artifice was plausible to bring the whole body into
the same predicament, with a man of Archbishop
Tenison's Moderation (for such that worthy Prelate really was) at their head.

But if a man of moderation, how shall we account for this scheme of Episcopal discipline espouf-
ed in this codicil, and on which the good old man
lays so much stress ? could he be ignorant that it
was

(o) Page 9.

was the exercife of. the fame powers from which
the original Colonifts of *America* fled into the
wildernefs ? On the other hand it may be afked,
could this be the fame man, who in the year 1689,
pleaded for admitting the diffenting Clergy into
the Church without reordination by Bifhops ?
Could this be the fame man, who had experienced
fo feverely in 1700, how improper Synodical af-
femblies were to regulate ecclefiaftical proceedings,
or to prevent and abate factions and divifions (*p*)?

.The truth is, this codicil was executed but
twelve days before the Archbifhop's death, when
the powers. of judgment and reflection may well
be fuppofed to have been greatly impaired. His
Grace was then in the eighty-fifth year of his age,
worn out with the effects of a fevere gout, and
other infirmities incident to fo late a period of life.
He was then alfo in the hands of two or three
reverend Doctors, who have fince had many opportunities of difplaying their attachment to the
Church in the moft eminent ftations, and who
would not fail to fuggeft to the expiring Prelate,
the merit 'and the glory of contributing to a
fcheme fo beneficial and fo honourable to the
Church of *England*. That this Archbifhop was
then under fome fuch influence, is highly probable from his mentioning in the codicil, that
" many of his brethren of the Propagating So-
c 4 " ciety,

(*p*) Memoirs of Archbifhop *Tenifon*, page 13, 14. and
77—101.

" ciety, were fenfible as well as himfelf of the
" neceffity of fettling Bifhops in *America*, for
" the *wife* ends there fignified ;" which naturally
refers to fome converfation on the fubject ftill
frefh in his mind, of which he retained the impreffions fo long at leaft as was neceffary to anfwer the purpofes of his advifers. But though
Archbifhop *Tenifon* had not remaining upon his
mind " thofe ftrong impreffions of the terrors of
" ecclefiaftical influence," fo prevalent " at the
" latter end of Queen *Anne*'s, and the beginning of
" King *George* the firft's reign ;" yet it feems
thofe impreffions ftill remained with " perfons
" in public ftations," which fufficiently accounts
for the hints in the codicil, *viz.* " the much im-
" portunity, and the many [unperformed] pro-
" mifes," of eftablifhing an Hierarchical jurisdiction and difcipline, in the north American Colonies. The Minifters, were aware of the characters of the *importuners*, though the honeft,
unfufpecting Archbifhop was not.

In one word, great allowances ought to be
made for the *failings* of fo great and fo good a
man as Archbifhop *Tenifon*, but nothing can be
more invidious, or more injurious to his character, than to hold them up as examples for imita-
tion.

To proceed. His Grace would have it believed, that " fome people have apprehended,
" that the appointment of American Bifhops will
" tend

" tend to the depreffion of the Hierarchy, as it
" will afford the Laity here an example of Englifh
" Bifhops abroad with no other than fpiritual
" powers; which may tempt them to think of
" reducing the Bifhops at home to the fame con-
" dition (*q*)."

Had his Grace thought proper to inform us
who they were that formed fuch apprehenfions,
we might poffibly have hit upon fome method of
fatisfying them, different from that his Grace
hath taken; which, it is not unlikely Mr
Walpole might confider as a fneer. If thefe apprehenders were fuch as my Lords the Bifhops
had convinced, that none but what his Grace
calls *fpiritual powers*, were to be granted to their
American brethren, it would be hard to fay what
melancholy confequences they might *not* draw
from a contemplation on the hardfhip and in-
dignity of fuch a limitation.

But to raife thefe drooping fpirits, his Grace
very comfortably affures them, that all is fafe and
fnug at home, as heart can wifh. " I fhould be
" very willing," fays his Grace, " for the bene-
" fit of thofe of our communion in the Colonies,
" to run a greater rifque than I conceive this to
" be." And the reafon of his Grace's fecurity on
this head was, it feems, that it is " no longer a
" fecret, that the *temporal* powers and privileges
.." of

(*q*) Letter to Mr *Walpole*. page 10.

" of my Lords the Bifhops, are merely concef-
" fions from the ftate (r)."

Here one would imagine, thefe *men of appre-*
henfion might afk, " But, the ftate obferving
" from the examples of American Bifhops that
" thefe temporal powers and privileges might be
" fpared, is there no danger, that it might take
" them away?" To this indeed his Grace gives
no anfwer, though Mr *Walpole* muft know he
had a very fubftantial one in *petto* ; namely, that
though the ftate *might* do this, yet as long as the
Bifhops, with thefe *powers* and *privileges* conti-
nued to make as *harmlefs* and *ufeful* a branch of
the conftitution as *many others*, they run no rifque
that the ftate ever *would*.

This was dextrous enough: for had this reafon been given, it would have occurred to another
fort of apprehenders, that the ftate might poffibly
think thefe temporal powers and privileges as
harmlefs and *ufeful* in the hands of American Prelates, as they are and have been in the hands of
their Lordfhips at home ; and in confequence of
that notion, would hereafter confer them ; an
apprehenfion which might have brought his
Grace's *fincerity* a third time in queftion. And
indeed I am fo far from thinking this *as unlikely
to happen as moft things*, that I cannot but be of
opinion, that, had *American* Bifhops been appointed about the time this Letter was written,

his

(r) Page 10.

his Grace would have lived to fee this event, and yet have been very able to juftify his *fincerity* by faying, " Pray, Gentlemen Colonifts, do not " blame me. I was very *fincere* in propofing to " limit your Bifhops to *fpiritual* powers : but who " am I, that you fhould expect *me* to control " the policy of the ftate?" Could Mr *Walpole* forbear ,fmiling at the management of his correfpondent ?

After an uncandid, not to fay, unjuft comparifon of the Church and State principles of the inferior, with thofe of the fuperior Clergy, and telling us, by way of ftriking the balance, " that " there never was a time known when the upper " part of the Clergy were fo univerfally free from " wild high Church notions (*s*)," his Grace, very incautioufly complains, that " the regard " which the bulk of the people *had* for religion, " and the teachers of it, is greatly diminifhed, " and diminifhing daily, to a degree," fays his Grace, " which I wonder wife men are not alarm- " ed at (*t*) ?"

.It had been well, his Grace had mentioned the time when the people *had* this *undiminifhed* regard for religion and the teachers of it, that both the fact and the reafons for it might have been afcertained

(*s*) Witnefs his Grace's *Lectures, Charges,* and *Synodal Oration,* and fome other performances, well known to have been fabricated under his Grace's patronage and infpection. .

(*t*) Page 12.

tained with precifion. The *bulk of the people* had, at a certain period, a moft *undiminifhed* regard for Dr *Henry Sacheverel*, and the fort of religion which he, and a number of other teachers, took care to inculcate. I would hope his Grace did not allude to thefe times, or to teachers like thefe. I would fuppofe thefe were the times of thofe *wild high Church notions*, which his Grace difclaims for himfelf and the upper part of his brethren. In what refpect then, does the regard of the bulk of the people for religion, and the teachers of it, appear to be diminifhed, in times fubfequent to thefe?

His Grace fhould by no means have left us in the dark on thefe heads, left it fhould be fufpected, either that this *diminifhed* regard is owing to fome default in the teachers, or that the teachers who complain of it, require more regard than is due to them. But it was more efpecially neceffary his Grace fhould have been more explicit on this article, as in the very next period his Grace feems to follicit an increafe of political power for the teachers of religion, in order to recover this diminifhed regard from the bulk of the people.

" It is as important, fays his Grace, even in a " *political* view, that they," [the teachers of religion] " fhould be able to do good, as that they " fhould not be able to do harm." A circumftance that is plainly recommended to the confideration

deration of thofe wife men, whó, to his Grace's furprife, are not alarmed at the prefent difregard of the teachers of religion.

Now in this *political* view, the teachers of religion cannot be enabled to do the good required, but by an increafe of political power. The fpiritual power of preaching the word of God, and of adminiftring with all diligence to the fpiritual welfare of their refpective flocks, none of the eftablifhed teachers of religion in this happy country can be fuppofed either to want, or not to employ under our excellent and *unalterable* ecclefiaftical fyftem. Some people indeed are apt to think that more good might be done in this fpiritual way, than *is* done; and will perhaps be ready to fay, let the teachers of religion, from the higheft to the loweft, firft try what good may be done towards recovering this regard of the people, by the ferious and diligent application of their fpiritual powers; and if this, upon a fair experiment, fhould be found to be infufficient, it will then be time enough to move for an increafe of their *political* power.

But what is extremely unfortunate for his Grace's argument, the Colonifts of our communion it feems, are in the fame predicament with the bulk of the people in old *England*.

" Nor do I find," adds his Grace, " that bi-
" gotry to the Church prevails among the mem-
" bers

" bers of it in our Colonies ;" (*u*) which can only fignify, (as that claufe falls in with what goes before) that, the regard of the bulk of the Church of *England* Colonifts for religion, and the teachers of it, is equally diminifhed among them, as in the mother country.

Will not then an increafe of political power be as neceffary for thefe new teachers of religion in *America*, as for the old ones at home ? And muft not their limited fpiritual powers be as ineffectual for a reformation there, as they have been found to be in *England ?*

" The Bifhop of *London*'s Commiffaries," his Grace believes, " have gained no acceffions to " what was granted them originally." (*w*) The contrary of which is the truth, as will be feen below. Not to mention, what has been often hinted, that the Commiffaries have frequently found the means, not only of pretending to, but of exercifing powers which never were granted them.

" But the Bifhops will be more narrowly " watched, by the Governors, by other Sects, by " the Laity, and even the Clergy of their own " communion." (*x*)

But what kind of men muft thefe Bifhops be who want fo much *watching*, and that by perfons fo differently interefted in their appointment? if his Grace knew that this would be the cafe, he

muft

muſt have known likewiſe, that it could only proceed from a *jealouſy*, entertained by the Coloniſts
of all ranks and denominations, of the natural
tendency of this Epiſcopal appointment to encroach-
ment and oppreſſion. And with theſe ſentiments,
how could his Grace imagine ſuch appointment
would ſtir up no *dangerous uneaſineſſes?* But indeed
when we conſider the different circumſtances to
which this variety of *watching* muſt be directed,
one cannot help ſuppoſing that *dangerous uneaſineſſes* muſt be the natural conſequence of this abundant vigilance.

The Governors would watch according to their
directions from home, which would probably be,
that the Biſhops (the confidants of the crown)
ſhould not ſuffer from any diminution of the regard that is due to them; the other ſects would
watch, on the contrary, that this regard ſhould
not ariſe above what they *imagine* is due to them,
which they would fix at a much lower ſtandard
than the Governors would think reaſonable; the
Laity would watch, that they might not be ha-
raſſed with Eccleſiaſtical cenſures; and the Clergy
would watch to inforce them, and to ſupport the
regard due to Epiſcopal Power; and in that they
would certainly find their account, as the Biſhops
muſt have the power of rewarding, or at leaſt of
recommending the meritorious, as well as cenſur-
ing delinquents.

However,

However, that the Bishops would be more narrowly watched than the Commissaries have been,
is contrary to all experience. A man would have
little chance for redress against the arbitrary acts of
a justice of the peace, who could not obtain satis-
faction for the insults of a petty constable. One
cannot but wonder his Grace should not feel the
ridicule to which this childish representation would
expose him.

The remainder of his Grace's lucubrations in
this paragraph, are built upon the same sort of
hypotheses; militating partly against matter of
fact, and partly against each other, as where he
speaks of "Governors *watching* the Bishops," who
" will nevertheless be such persons as the Crown
" *can best confide in* (*y*)." Might not his Grace
as well have said, that the *Governors* would be
more narrowly watched by the *Bishops?* and again
" a right of recalling them may be reserved to the
" King." Does his Grace mean, a right of putting an end to their function? so it should seem
as, *ex hypothesi*, this *recalling* must be on account
of their misdemeanours. It is a *material* question,
and I should like to see an answer to it, from some
of those to whom his Grace has bequeathed his
principles on the article of Church Authority.

His Grace having done his endeavour to quiet
our apprehensions with respect to an increase of
Church Power among the Americans, by lending
them

(*y*) Page 13.

them Bishops, on mere suppositions and probabi-
lities, proceeds to strengthen his case by referring
to actual precedents!

" It ought to be considered further, says his
" Grace, that an Act of the last session of Parlia-
" ment [1749] which passed without any opposition
" from any body, hath *expressly established* Mo-
" RAVIAN Bishops in *America*, who have much
" higher and stricter notions of Church Govern-
" ment and Discipline than we have (z)."

Bold and surprizing! His Grace ventures no
less than the supposition that Mr *Walpole* must never have seen the Act in question, nor have known
any thing of the contents of it.

Can any Man of common Sense understand less
by the words, *expressly established*, than that the
Act gives these Moravian Bishops a power to exercise their function, assigns them their stations,
and secures their stipends?

And yet the case is only this. The *Moravians*,
to whom this Act relates, are such as scruple to
take an oath, or to serve personally in the army.
This Law dispenses with them in both these Ar-
ticles, upon condition of their making a solemn af-
firmation instead of an oath, and paying a sum of
money sufficient to hire a substitute to perform mi-
litary service in their room.

But lest the Government should be imposed upon
by persons pretending to be of the *Moravian* So-
D   ciety

(z) Page 14.

ciety who are not, it is enacted, that every one who claims the benefit of this act, shall produce a certificate signed by some Bishop of the said Church, or by the Pastor of such Church or Congregation who shall be nearest to the place where the claim is made, that he is actually a member of the said Church.

And to prevent frauds or forgeries of false certificates, it is farther enacted, that the advocate of the said Church, shall lay or cause to be laid before the Commissioners for Trade and Plantations a list or lists of all the Bishops of the said Church who are appointed by them to grant certificates as aforesaid, together with their hand-writing and usual seal, and the names hand-writing and seals of any Bishops that shall hereafter be consecrated by them, as aforesaid; and the names of such Pastors, as shall be authorised by the said Advocate or Bishops to give certificates in any of his Majesty's Colonies in *America* (a).

Undoubtedly his Grace might give what names to what things he pleased, and so might call this an Act for establishing *Moravian* Bishops in *America*. But we are not obliged to adopt his Grace's ideas. It is not even said that these certifying Bishops should be resident in *America*; and for any thing that appears, they might be such as resided in *England*, *Poland*, *Prussia*, *Silesia*, &c. in all which, and in other places, the Act says, the Moravian Church is settled; and these Bishops indeed are

(a) 22d GEORGE II. cap. 30.

are juft as *exprefsly eftablifhed* by this Act, in thofe countries, as in *America*.

His Grace affirms, that this Act was paffed without any oppofition from any body. But, *Rimius*, the virulent chaftifer of the Moravians, affures us it was oppofed by a certain member, upon a fuggeftion, that " the Moravians in *Germany* had " made the greateft part of Proteftants run mad " by their devices." When he could not prevail to have the Bill thrown out, the fame perfon propofed that they fhould be reftrained from making converts; which was likewife difregarded, for a reafon which fhall be mentioned by and by (*b*).

" Why then" fays his Grace (arguing a *fortiori*) " fhould there be fuch fear of eftablifhing Bifhops " of the Church of *England?*"

A queftion which fuppofes thefe *Moravian* Bifhops were eftablifhed with the knowledge and confent of the Colonifts; which every one knows could not be the cafe; and in all probability this Act was paffed, before the *Americans* knew that any fuch thing was thought of. And even with refpect to our own people at home, Bifhop *Lavington*, who knew as much of what paffed in parliament as his brother of *Oxford*, informs us, that " the fettlement of the *Moravians* in thefe King- " doms feems to have been obtained *furreptitiously*, " under pretence of their being a peaceable inno-

D 2 " cent

(*b*) Preface to the Supplement to the Candid Narrative, *page* cxvii.

" cent fort of people." But his Lordſhip hoped
that " their iniquity and filthineſs being laid open
" by Mr *Rimius* and himſelf, they would be com-
" pelled to emigrate, as had been found neceſſary
" in other countries (*b*)."

Doubtleſs his Grace's argument *a fortiori* hath
great force and propriety, in reference to this precedent.

His Grace's expoſtulation indeed is founded on
the conſideration, that " the Moravians have much
" higher and ſtricter notions of Church Govern-
" ment and Diſcipline, than we of the Church of
" *England* have." Well then, let us conſider
what ſort of Biſhops theſe Moravians have among
them.

The *Unitas fratrum*, in whoſe favour the Act
under conſideration was made, are ſaid there, to
be members of the Church which was formerly
ſettled in *Moravia* and *Bohemia*: the remains of
which was then ſettled in *Poland*. Among theſe
Count *Zinzendorf* was ordained, or if you pleaſe,
conſecrated a Biſhop at *Liſſa*. But here, " all
" their Miniſters were on an equal footing, the
" oldeſt of them, without having reſpect to the
" importance of his cure, is always choſen a ſe-
" nior or elder for the ſake of Ordinations, and
" is nothing elſe but *primus inter pares*, having
" not the leaſt juriſdiction or authority over the
" other

(*b*) Preface to the *Moravians* Compared, *page* xiv.

" other Clergy (c)." This gives us no very ftriking idea of the high-Church notions of thefe *Moravians* with refpect to Church Government and
Difcipline. And would the Englifh Bifhops defigned
for *America*, confent to a reduction of this kind,
perhaps the Colonifts might give the project a farther confideration.

But fuppofing the *Moravian* Bifhops to be exprefsly eftablifhed in *America*, and to have all the
prelatical powers with which our Englifh Bifhops
are invefted, what is the confequence? A very
unfortunate one for his Grace's project, if Mr
Rimius is to be believed, who when he wanted to
exclude the *Moravian* Bifhops from exercifing their
function in *England*, confronted them with a *Canon*
of the firft *Nicene* Council, which enjoins, that two
Bifhops fhall not prefide together in the fame city.
The *Moravian* Bifhops, according to this doctrine,
have a canonical title by *preoccupation*, and the
Englifh Bifhops muft be excluded of courfe from
America, on the pain of being cenfured as unca-
nonical interlopers.

" If for want of thefe" [Englifh Bifhops] con-
tinues his Grace, " the *Moravian* Bifhops fhould
" ordain fuch Minifters for our people as they
" thought proper, or fhould they, by adminis-
" tring confirmation, or by the reverence of their
" Epifcopal Character, be continually gaining

converts

(c) Rimius ubi fupra, *p.* xxxi.

" converts from us, it would be a very undefire-
" able thing on many accounts, particularly on
" this, that moſt of them refuſe taking oaths, and
" bearing arms."

Had I been of counſel with the publiſhers of
this Letter, I ſhould certainly have adviſed them
to have ſuppreſſed this paſſage, unleſs they could
have added a note to ſhew that theſe converſions
had actually been made by the *Moravians* in
alarming numbers, and that undeſireable conſe-
quences had proceeded from them. As matters now turn out, this idle ſcarecrow is con-
ſigned to contempt and ridicule by the experience
of twenty years, during which no ſuch events have
been heard of.

But this is not the worſt. His Grace, by this
unwary auguration is expoſed to a very obvious reflection, namely, that " a power of ordaining and
" confirming, together with the reverence of the
" Epiſcopal Character, are very likely means of
" continually gaining proſelytes." And what
was *undeſireable* with reſpect to theſe *Moravian*
Biſhops in his Grace's account, we may be ſure
would be *undeſireable* in the account of the Non-
conforming Coloniſts, with reſpect to Biſhops of
the Church of *England.* They will therefore conſider this inſinuation as the effect of his Grace's in-
advertently dropping the maſk, and as exhibiting
a full view of his expectations from the eſtabliſhment of Biſhops in *America.*

But

But after all, on what accounts would these conversions be undesireable? one would have expected from an English Prelate to have had *one* of these accounts at least specified, as affecting the *religion* of the converts, *viz.* the *undesireableness* of having our people converted from a *better* religion to a *worse*. But then, what must have been said for Archbishop *Potter*, who, in a complementary Letter to Count *Zinzendorf*, so highly extols the orthodoxy of the *Moravian* Church; " acknow-
" ledging its full agreement with the Church of
" *England*, both in the purity of the primitive
" faith, and in the defence of the primitive dif-
" cipline?" and if Dr *Potter* was *sincere* in this, we may be very sure that how high and strict soever the notions of the Moravians may be concerning Church Government and Discipline, they are neither higher nor stricter than the notions of the Church of *England* on those subjects, if a learned and orthodox Archbishop of *Canterbury* may determine for her (*d*).

It was mentioned above, that when the act in favour of the Moravians was under the consideration of Parliament, a certain member who opposed it, not being able to prevail to have it thrown out, proposed to have them restrained from making converts. This was likewise rejected, " the
" majority" says *Rimius*, " taking these people

D 4 " for

(*d*) Biographia Britannica, vol. vii. Art. *Zinzendorf*, Rem. [G.]

" for the ancient Moravian Church." Which af-
fords another reafon why his Grace (to whom
this tranfaction could hardly be unknown) would
not mention the converfions made by the Moravians as undefireable on a *religious* account, as the
parliament had feemed to determine, that the religious principles of the Americans would not be
hurt by their being converted to the *Moravian*
fyftem.

His Grace's political reafon for ftanding in
awe of thefe *converfions*, would, I fuppofe, be lefs
confiderable with Mr *Walpole*, as nothing *undefireable*, of this fort at leaft, had arofe from the
Penfylvanian Quakers, who profefs the fame principles with thefe *Moravians*.

The nonjuring *Jacobite* Bifhops in our Colonies, we may well fuppofe to be mere nonentities,
as his Grace himfelf is fo very doubtful about
them.

"" But popifh Bifhops alfo," his Grace apprehends, " have recourfe to the Colonies from time
" time. At leaft," fays. his Grace, " the Bifhop
" of *Quebec* hath no fmall influence in a very
" important new fettlement of ours." (*e*)

A fhrewd writer in the *London* Chronicle of
Auguft 22, feems difpofed to believe, from the
mention here made of this *new* fettlement, that
this Letter to Mr *Walpole* is certainly *fpuricus*,
as this fettlement was not *ours* till eight years
after

(*e*) Letter, page 15.

after the date of it. To which might be added, that from the time this fettlement became *ours*, till after the peace of *Fontainbleau*, there was no popifh Bifhop at *Quebec*. Nor indeed could this claufe be pen'd, unlefs by the fpirit of prophecy, till the year 1764, when the prefent popifh Bifhop of *Quebec*, embarked in *England* for his new diocefe, where he could have no perfonal influence, great or fmall, before his arrival.

But inftead of relying upon this as a proof that this Letter is fpurious, I am inclined to think it more probable, that his Grace thought proper to *retouch* this favourite refcript from time to time; retrenching poffibly fome topics he had made ufe of in his anfwer to Dr *Mayhew*'s obfervations, and adding others, as new incidents arofe relative to his fubject. Of this there are, if I miftake not, evident traces in other parts of this Letter, though none perhaps which afford fo manifeft indications of *a mind fympathizing with bodily infirmities*.

For might not his Grace have been afked, How came this Bifhop of *Quebec* by his no fmall influence? How came he there at all? Was not the *eftablifhment* of a popifh Bifhop in an important new fettlement under his Majefty's government, a matter worthy of the interpofition of a proteftant Archbifhop? Was not his Grace then at the head of the Church of *England?* And was it ever heard that his Grace remonftrated either

in

in public or private, againſt a meaſure ſo ſeemingly inconſiſtent with the intereſts and honour of the Church of *England*, and even with the ſafety of our proteſtant government?

This is not the firſt time I have heard theſe queſtions aſked; and I wiſh I could ſay I had ever heard a more ſatisfactory anſwer to them, than that the profound ſilence obſerved on that occaſion, was with a view to obtain a precedent for ſettling Church of *England* Biſhops in *America.*

But whatever might be the reaſon of his Grace's *acquieſcence* at that period, certain it is that the toleration of a popiſh Biſhop at *Quebec*, has been brought as an argument for eſtabliſhing proteſtant Biſhops in the Colonies, in certain diſcourſes delivered before a certain Society, where his Grace preſided; and in this very pamphlet his Grace was not aſhamed to plead the example of popiſh Biſhops at home, who, he tells us, " perform the ſame religious acts by *connivance,* " which he propoſes his *American* Biſhops ſhould " be impowered to do by authority." (*f*)

Can theſe precedents be *decently* pleaded by the fathers of the Church of *England* for eſtabliſhing proteſtant Biſhops in *America*, but upon the ſuppoſition that the toleration of popiſh Biſhops is abſolutely void of danger, both here and in *America* ?

(*f*) Ibid. page 19.

America? And yet, to ferve the fame turn another way, his Grace, moft inconfiftently fuppofes
the danger from the influence of the Bifhop of
Quebec to be great, and ftill greater from the
neglect of not having Bifhops of our own in that
country to counteract this influence. Which
however, is an hypothefis contrary to a known
fact. For to what can this counteraction amount
in the Colonies where a popifh Bifhop is permitted by more than *connivance,* when, as we learn
from his Grace on another occafion, *popifh Bifhops refide here and perform every part of their
function without offence and without obfervation,* (g)
in fpite of the vigilance of twenty-fix Prelates of
the eftablifhed Church, and the terror of ftrict
laws, wifely provided by our proteftant anceftors
againft the pernicious effects of the intolerant fpirit and deftructive principles of thofe very
Bifhops.

We are now arrived at the third queftion, *viz.*
" Whether fuch an appointment, however harm-
" lefs and ufeful it might be otherwife, would
" not ftir up dangerous uneafineffes, abroad or
" at home? And here," fays his Grace, " it is
" afked, If the members of our Church in
" *America,* would like to have Bifhops among
" them, why they never petitioned for them?" (b)
This queftion, without all doubt, came from

Mr

(g) Anfwer to Dr *Mayhew's* obfervations, page 66.
(b) Letter, page 15.

Mr *Walpole*, and therefore we may safely take it for granted, that no petition for Bifhops had ever been offered on the part of thefe Church of *England* Colonifts. It will be neceffary to give his Grace's anfwer to it in his own words.

" Surely their omitting it may well be afcribed " in part, to the thoughtlefsnefs of mankind " about their religious concerns, which hath been " fo peculiarly great in thofe countries, that fome " of them did not petition for help, when they " had no one office of Chriftianity adminiftred " among them." (*i*)

Turn over the leaf, and there you will find it thus written, " Indeed of courfe it fhould be pre- " fumed, and none but the very ftrongeft evi- " dence admitted to the contrary, that all perfons " defire to have within their reach, the means " of exercifing their religion completely." (*k*)

What is now to be done to reconcile the *fact* to the *prefumption?* We are to prefume, that *all perfons* defire, what the thoughtlefsnefs of man-kind, and ftrong evidence from a moft remark-able cafe to confirm it, plainly fhew that *all perfons* do not defire.

Take the matter of fact, and you find the Church of *England* Colonifts in fo abandoned a ftate of negligence and indolence about their re-ligious concerns, that there is not the leaft proba-bility that a whole bench of Bifhops would recall

them

(*i*) Ibid.   (*k*) Page 16.

them to a due attention. For it appears by the sequel, that miffionaries have been fent them unpetitioned for, without the leaft good effect. They continue as thoughtlefs about their religious concerns as ever, as appears from their not petitioning to have the complete exercife of their religion within their reach.

Take the prefumption, and you muft conclude they are perfuaded that they already have within their reach the means of exercifing their religion completely without Bifhops; and that his Grace was only inventing reafons for their not petitioning fuitable to his own ideas.

I fhall not inquire into the matter of fact, namely, how far any part of the Colonies, was ever without the adminiftration of any one office of Chriftianity among them: I have been told, it is not true; but be that as it may, I have his Grace's own teftimony before me, given when he was Bifhop of *Oxford*, that they who were in the moft deplorable circumftances of this fort, were not flack in petitioning for relief.

. " In thefe circumftances," faid the Bifhop of *Oxford*, " the poor inhabitants made from ALL PARTS
" the moft affecting reprefentations of their de-
" plorable condition, the truth of which was but
" too fully confirmed by their refpective Go-
" vernors, and the perfons of principal note
" among

" among them *." In this variety of his Grace's accounts, what are we to believe?

Another reafon why thefe Colonifts did not petition, is, that " probably too many of their " Clergy think, they may both live more negli- " gently, and have a better chance for prefer- " ment now, than if a Bifhop were to infpect " them, and ordain natives to be their ri- " vals." (*l*)

This may be a reafon why thefe negligent, afpiring, envious Clergymen, fhould *not* petition, but is rather a reafon why the Laity *fhould*, efpecially if " they defire to have within their reach, " the means of exercifing their religion *com-* " *pletely* ;" for this they can no more have under negligent paftors, than they can have it without Bifhops. But indeed, if the Lay-Colonifts took their meafures from experience and hiftory, they would hardly think the negligence or ambition of their paftors were likely to be cured by petitioning for Bifhops. It is hardly to be fuppofed

---

* See the Bifhop of *Oxford's* Sermon before the Society for the *Propagation*, &c. *Feb.* 1740—41. page 5. fecond edition, octavo. It is certain that *all parts* of our American Colonies, were never in this deplorable condition, and that any reprefentations of that fort muft be falfe, unlefs, by a mean and difreputable equivocation, the preacher meant, that the offices adminiftred by the non-conformift paftors, are *not* offices of Chriftianity. Confult Dr *Mayhew's* obfervations on the charter and conduct, &c. chapters v. and vi.

(*l*) Letter, page 15.

pofed but thefe Colonifts muft have fome concep-
tion how matters have ftood in the mother country in former times, as well as in the prefent.
They muft be aware, that there have been times,
at no great diftance from the migration of their
anceftors to *America*, when the Bifhops of *England* were deprived of their power.   The prefent
age, wherein the Bifhops of the mother country
enjoy their power under the protection of the
ftate and the law, they have before them in full
contemplation;   and they may if they pleafe,
compare the diligence, humility, and fimplicity
of common paftors and minifters of the Church
at thefe different periods.   They will at leaft
perceive, that there were more temptations to
negligence and ambition in the one fituation,
than in the other. Commendams, difpenfations
for pluralities, and fine-cures, (the parents of non-
refidence, and the lures of ecclefiaftical ambition)
are appendages to Epifcopal Churches, and, as
fome people imagine, fubftantial obftructions to
chriftian edification. There is a chance at leaft
that religion would be upon a better footing
where the Clergy have not thefe indulgences to
look for : and they who are negligent and am-
bitious without them, would hardly be more diligent or lefs afpiring when they are thrown in
their way.

At length his Grace fuggefts a third reafon to
Mr *Walpole* why thefe Colonifts did not petition

for Bifhops, which is, that " the inhabitants
" of the Colonies, living at fuch a diftance, and
" not knowing when an Application to the Go-
" vernment might be feafonable; and being
" affured, that the Bifhops here, efpecially the
" Bifhop of *London*, and the Society for Pro-
" pagating the Gofpel, would always be atten-
" tive to this point, have left it to them. And
" they to whom it is thus left, have received abun-
" dant proofs, that very great numbers of the
" Laity of the Church of *England*, in thofe coun-
" tries, of higher as well as lower rank, *earneſtly*
" *deſire* to have Bifhops fettled there, and think
" it would be a moſt valuable public benefit (*m*)."

But how comes it that Mr *Walpole*, a minifter
of ftate, fhould never know of all this? How
comes it, that the Bifhops and the Society to whom
this matter was left, with fo full confidence, that
they would always be attentive to it, never either
petitioned the Government themfelves on behalf
of thofe who put this confidence in them, or apprifed the Government of the earneft defires of
thefe Colonifts to have Bifhops fettled among them?

Whatever his Grace might do, I am perfuaded Mr *Walpole* did not quibble upon the word, *petition*; but affuredly meant that it never appeared
to the Government, that the Colonifts had any
fuch *earneſt deſires* to have a Bifhop among them:
and that whatever had been laid before the Government

(*m*) Letter, page 16.

ment by the Bishops and the Society, of this sort, had fallen short of the proof that was required.

The real truth, I believe, is, that the missionaries have been from time to time instructed to use their endeavours to procure such petitions from the Colonists, in which some of them have not been remiss, as appears sufficiently by Dr *Bradbury Chandler*'s Pamphlets. But, as it should seem, without any effect, except perhaps, some intimations from their Governors and Counsellors who are appointed in them other country. Every one knows, that his Grace, after his accession to the See of *Canterbury*, was particularly assiduous in promoting an Episcopal establishment in *America*, in which pious project, Mr *Apthorp* and the said Dr *Chandler* seem to have been his most considerable instruments. And as no body ever heard of these *earnest desires* of the Colonists to give into this scheme so early as the year 1750, before the notice given us in this Letter, it is probable his Grace might have been privately at work on this project, from the moment he was invested with the lawn. Whether he had any coadjutors, after the demise of Bp *Gibson*, (from whom most probably he derived his *entetement* for this Measure) I cannot say; but from that period the Bishop of *Oxford* was undoubtedly the master workman, and knew more of the pains that had been taken at home and abroad to carry the point of petitioning, than any of his brethren. But unfortunately Mr *Walpole* happened to know

E   as

as much as the Bishop of *Oxford*; who, for want
of the *abundant proof* that Mr *Walpole* had reason
to demand, is obliged to fly to the miserable expedient of *presuming* upon, what he had himself
before shewn to be contrary to the matter of fact.

But tho' this affair of *petitioning* could not be
brought about, yet his Grace informs us, that
" the Bishops and the Society, to whom this mat-
" ter was left, had found no cause to imagine that
" any opposition would be made to it from that
" quarter(*o*) " Which is cautiously enough
worded, and perhaps implies no more, than that
it was more reasonable for them to believe the accounts transmitted to them by their own Missionaries, than those which came from any other quarter.

" It is true," says his Grace, " some of them
" have provided against enlarging the jurisdic-
" tion of the Commissaries ; but none of them
" have expressed any *public reluctance* to the ap-
" pointment of Bishops(*p*)."

Some of them ; i.e. of the lay Colonists of the
Church of *England*. But these, whoever they
were, could not thus *provide* without some public
act of the whole body, or of the whole representative. Whence I suppose the Government would
easily conceive with what reluctance they would
listen to the appointment of a superior power,

when

(*o*) Page 16.   (*p*) Page 17.

when they had been so careful to provide against
the oppreſſion of an inferior (q).

If

(q) How they were diſpoſed towards the appointment of
Biſhops, about this time, may be underſtood from the following anecdote. In *May* 1749, *Eliakim Palmer* Eſq; introduced
Mr *Hooper* (one of the Council of *Barbadoes*, poſſeſſed of a conſiderable plantation there) to the Biſhop of *London* [Dr *Sherlock*].
Mr *Hooper*, on that occaſion, told his Lordſhip, that " he and
all their people diſliked the project." He informed his Lordſhip likewiſe, that his Lordſhip's Commiſſary there, requeſted
an Act to impower him to ſuſpend ſuch Clergymen as were infamous in their lives. One Clergyman of unexceptionable
character, oppoſed it, and ſo the power was granted for three
years only. One of the firſt acts of this Commiſſary was, to
enſnare this good man. At a public meeting they put an ingredient into his punch, to make him drunk. So ſoon as he
found himſelf not well, he quitted the place, and went home-
ward. His way was through a long narrow paſſage. There
they placed a common whore, who, as inſtructed, clung about
him, with other indecencies. The good man however ſhook
her off, and went directly home. They had placed two men
about this narrow paſſage to obſerve what paſſed. The next
day he received a ſummons to appear before the Commiſſary,
to a charge of being drunk and picking up a whore, and taking her into that paſſage to gratify his luſt. The two men
witneſſed againſt him, and the Commiſſary ſuſpended him.
The whole pariſh were diſſatisfied, and applied to the Commiſſary to take off the ſuſpenſion, but he refuſed. They then
applied to the Governor and Council to uſe their intereſt with
the Commiſſary, that he might be reſtored to them. They
did ſo, but to no purpoſe. The people, nettled at this refuſal,
demanded a libel againſt another Clergyman of an infamous
and profligate character. The charge was proved, but the
Commiſſary did not exerciſe his power; for this latter was at

E z   the

If the Colonifts expreffed no *public reluctance* to
the appointment of Bifhops among them, it was a
teftimony of their good fenfe and prudent caution,
as no *public attempt* had been made towards fuch
an appointment. His Grace indeed fays, that,
" for above forty years paft, the inhabitants there
" muft have had frequent notices, by various
" ways,

the head of thofe who requefted the Court to grant the power.
When Mr *Hooper* had told this ftory to the Bifhop, he added,
" And now, my Lord, will you fend a Bifhop to us, who
" will have this, and greater powers?" His Lordfhip anfwered, *It is not I that fend Bifhops to* America, *it is the Society
for Propagating the Gofpel in foreign Parts, who are the movers
of this matter.* Mr *Hooper* replied, " I do not care who are
" the movers, but this I can with confidence affure your Lord-
" fhip, that if ever a Bifhop fets foot on our Ifland, the people
" will tofs him into the Sea." This fo affected the Bifhop,
that he told thofe concerned, they had beft drop the defign of
fending a Bifhop to the Sugar-Iflands, for thofe people were
too hot to be dealt with, and ftick only to the other part of
the propofal, *viz.* to fend one to the Continent. In confequence, Letters were written to *Virginia*, to get Letters from
thence, requefting a Bifhop might be fent there. But a Gentleman concerned for that Colony in *England*, being aware of
this fecret negociation, immediately wrote to one of the principal Gentlemen of the Council there; by which means the project was difappointed for that time. It will, I fuppofe, hardly
be doubted that the Bifhop of *Oxford* was at that time *one of
thofe concerned* in this Epifcopizing fcheme; and yet, he cannot be fuppofed, to have witten this Letter under a confciouf-
nefs of thefe facts, without the utmoft difingenuity: not to
mention, that he could not fuppofe but Mr *Walpole* muft know
enough

" ways, that such a design was in agitation." *p. 17.*
Possibly they had; but these were notices only of
secret cabals and intrigues of particular persons,
and perhaps some private application to men in
power. But while the design was kept private,
and confided to a trusty junto, the rest were at
liberty to deny it, and then, what would the Colonists

---

enough of these proceedings to be able to contradict him.
And therefore to save Dr *Secker* the reputation of his *sincerity,*
we must conclude, that my Lord of *London* did not choose to
communicate to him the particulars of the intelligence he received from Mr *Hooper,* or to make him privy to his Lordship's
correspondence with Mr *Walpole.* We see, Bishop *Sherlock*
disclaimed having any particular share in sending Bishops to
America, and lays the project to the account of the Propagating
Society, where no doubt he had observed the Bishop of *Oxford's*
headlong zeal for accomplishing this measure at all events;
and being a man of infinitely more prudence, as well as abilities, than Dr *Secker,* he determined to have no more to do
with him in this affair, than was unavoidable, as a Member
of the Propagating Society. The Editors probably thought it
might be giving some consequence to his Grace, to represent
him in the Advertisement, as going hand in hand with Bishop
Sherlock in this Episcopizing project, and might hope that the
inconsistency of this representation with what his Grace hath
recorded in the first page of his Letter, would be overlooked
by his Grace's friends and admirers. But have they not rather
given occasion to suspect by this piece of art, that his Grace
had no more consequence with Mr *Walpole,* than with Bishop
Sherlock? And that however his Grace came by a sight of that
Gentleman's Letter to Bishop *Sherlock,* his pretended Answer
to it was never out of the confines of his study till the memo-
rable year 1769?

lonifts have got by their *public reluctance?* Even the honour of being laughed at for trufting to uncertain rumours, and fighting with a fhadow?

His Grace next proceeds to quiet the apprehenfions of thofe who might be made uneafy by the confideration of the expence required to maintain thefe colony Bifhops, and tells us, " it is not in-" tended to burden the Crown or the fubject with " it." *p.* 17.

As if the gifts and contributions, mentioned juft after by his Grace, would be no burden upon the fubject? Some families muft want what is thus given and contributed, for what they will think, perhaps, more neceffary ufes. How often have we had Briefs for the purpofe of fupporting the Society's unmitred miffionaries? And would his Grace have infured us, that none of thefe would be circulated for the nobler purpofe of fupporting the dignity of Bifhops? And are thefe no burden to the fubject?

But where was his Grace's memory, where was the modefty of the Editors of this Letter, who could let fuch a declaration pafs, after Dr *Thomas Bradbury Chandler* had been at the pains to calculate *how inconfiderable* a tax upon the Americans would be, to maintain a requifite number of American Bifhops? And how fcurvily does this Dr come off, (when preffed upon this head by Dr *Chauncey*) with a filly quibbling diftinction between, " what it " would be *equitable* to pay," and " what, no " man, if he denied to pay, would deferve to be " confidered

" confidered in the light of a good fubject, or
" member of Society (r)."

His Grace, after acknowledging that the Pres-
byterians and Independents of *New England*, have
fignified their *diflike* of his project *of late*, conde-
fcends to fay, that, " there never was any thought
" of placing them there." *p.* 18.

How does this agree with Bifhop *Sherlock's* ex-
hortation, " to ftick to the propofal of fending a Bi-
" fhop to the continent?" But whatever his Grace's
thoughts might be in 1750, it is certain that *New
England*, after his promotion to *Canterbury*, was
the principal object of his Grace's cares ·for Epifcopal reformation in *America*. However, fo tender
was he of giving thefe people offence at the time he
was writing to Mr *Walpole*, that his Grace is
pleafed to allow, that " if they fhould object
" againft Bifhops coming occafionally to officiate
" amongft

(r) *The Appeal defended, or, the propofed* American *Epifcopate
vindicated, in anfwer to the objections and mifreprefentations of*
Dr Chauncey *and others.* By Thomas Bradbury Chandler,
D.D. *New York*, printed by *Hugh Gaine*, at the Bible and
Crown, in *Hanover Square*, 1769. p. 249, 250. Whoever will be
at the pains to compare this *Defence* with Dr *Secker's* Letter to Mr
Walpole, will very ferioufly lament Dr *Chandler's* misfortune in
being ftationed *three thoufand miles* from his Bifhop, by whofe
inftructions the *Appeal* was written, and for whofe honour it
was to be defended. He might otherwife have avoided the
mortification of feeing his high pretenfions to the rights and
privileges of the American Epifcopate, fo remarkably· con-
trafted with his Grace's humble conceffions, in an hour of
defpondency.

" amongft thofe of the Epifcopal perfuafion in
" that province, — *that* might be omitted."

Now it is well known, that the Society's Miffionaries in *New England* have always been more,
in a double proportion at leaft, than in the other
provinces in *America*. In the year 1761, about
thirty Miffionaries were ftationed in *New England*,
while in *New York*, *New Jerfey*, *Penfylvania*,
North Carolina, *South Carolina*, *Georgia*, the *Ba-
hama Iflands*, and *Barbadoes*, there were no more
than forty-nine, according to the Society's *Ab-
ftraĉts.* (s)

If then, notwithftanding the reafonablenefs of
the propofal in the abftraĉt, notwithftanding what
belongs to the nature of Epifcopal Churches, and
the indifpenfable neceffity of Confirmation to the
complete exercife of their religion ; notwithftanding
the neceffity of overlooking the conduĉt of *vagabond ftrangers*, fo indifferently qualified, as his
Grace reprefents many of them to be, — If, I fay,
notwithftanding all thefe confiderations, the perfonal miniftrations of a Bifhop in *New England*,
where there are thirty Epifcopal Churches, may
be omitted, it feems fcarce worth the while to
fend Bifhops, with the expenfive appointments,
fuitable to the dignity of their charaĉter, to prefide over forty-nine Miffionaries difperfed in eight
extenfive provinces, where even the fingle ceremony of Confirmation, to be completely exercifed,

(s) *Mayhew*'s Obfervations, page 45. *London* edition.

cifed, could hardly be performed by the labours of ten or a dozen Bifhops, if the uninftructed Negroes are to be taken into the account.

After all, his Grace feems to be confcious, that the true queftions would come to this, Whether dangerous uneafineffes would not be ftirred up in the Colonies, by the appointment of Bifhops? And whether the Colonifts would not have fufficient grounds for their uneafineffes, from their experience of the incroaching nature of Epifcopacy?

In anfwer to this latter queftion, his Grace thinks fit to fay, that the Colonifts, " cannot fail to " know how much the Epifcopal power exercifed " heretofore by Bifhops, hath long fince been " leffened, and the inclinations and principles of " thofe who are intrufted with it, altered for the " better." (t) This hath been confidered before, and we need only refer for an anfwer to it, to the paffage quoted above from his Grace's *Oratio Synodalis.* Let us add however, as this matter is once more come upon the carpet, that what his Grace afcribes to the *better inclinations and principles* of himfelf and his contemporary brethren, is confidered by other ftanch Churchmen, as an unhappy relaxation of that ancient difcipline, which the Church wifhes, in one of her offices, to have reftored. Of this complexion is the zealous Dr *Thomas Bradbury Chandler*, whom every one now underftands to fpeak the *real, undifguifed* fenfe,

(t) Page 18.

fenfe of Dr *Secker*, both in the *Appeal*, and in his *Defence* of it.

" The want of primitive difcipline in the
" Church at home," faith this diligent Miffionary,
" is no proof that the want of it is not ftill greater
" in the Colonies, nor that the want cannot in
" fome degree, be remedied by the propofed
" Epifcopate. We think that a ftrict difcipline,
" with regard to the American Clergy, might
" be exercifed under an Epifcopate. *This is cer-*
" *tainly expected.* IT IS AN IMPORTANT PART
" OF OUR PLAN ; and that American Bifhops
" would difappoint us in this refpect, none have
" a right to declare, until the experiment fhall
" have been made."(*u*)

Why no indeed, worthy Doctor, I dare fay the Colonifts have no fuch fufpicion; and therefore, I prefume, it is, that they are fo unwilling, and with great reafon, to have the experiment made. How little was this ftrenuous champion aware, while he was writing this, that fome of his fellow pupils at home were convincing the world, that there was a time, when their common patron had denied every word of it ; and that in fpite of his *Oratio Synodalis*, this denial was agreeable to his dying fentiments ? After this, truft, ye Colonifts, if you can, to the fincerity of thofe who folicit an *American* Epifcopate. None of you can be at a lofs to know what a high-flying Epifcopalian means by *primitive difcipline*, while the hiftory

(*u*) *Appeal defended*, page 103.

hiſtory of the ſettlement of your anceſtors in A-
merica remains. None of you can be ignorant,
that the *juriſdiction* required to carry *this primitive
diſcipline* into execution, muſt be as different from
the *plan* delineated in this Letter, as your own
plan is from that of Archbiſhop *Laud.* For
while his Grace is aſſuring you, that, " no more
" authority is deſired for American Biſhops, than
" the diſſenting Miniſters exerciſe here by law,
" or popiſh Prieſts and Biſhops by connivance:"
Dr *Chandler,* whoſe inſtructions are of a later
date, betrays his own and his party's *expectations,*
that *a ſtrict primitive diſcipline, with reſpect to the*
American *Clergy,* without diſtinction, may be
exerciſed under this new Epiſcopate.

Attending his Grace to *page* 19, we find ſome-
thing like an apology for the propagating Society's
ſending Letters into *America.* One would wiſh
to know, what circumſtance of Mr *Walpole*'s Letter, gave occaſion to it. Making due allowances
for his Grace's palliations and gloſſes, the caſe
ſeems to have been this. The zealous promoters
of *American* Epiſcopacy in the Society, finding
that the want of petitions from the Colonies was
a conſiderable obſtruction to the project, ſent
Letters privately to their confidants to procure
ſuch teſtimonies, (*viz.* that the Coloniſts approved
the meaſure) as might be a balance at leaſt
againſt the aſſurances the government had received, that they were averſe to it. The practice
came to be detected, and the alarm being taken

by

by the friends of religious liberty; the too probable confequences of it were remonftrated to the
government.　This brought fome *blame* upon
the contrivers of this fecret correfpondence, which
his Grace fought here to ward off, as well as he
could; modeftly requefting in the end, that the
government would permit them to play out their
game, before they rejected the propofal.

His Grace's next endeavour is to take off Mr
Walpole's apprehenfions, that the attempt, and
much more the execution of fuch a project,
" would raife animofities at home, produce de-
" clamations in pulpits, controverfies in pam-
" phlets, debates in parliament, revive the diftinc-
" tions of high and low among Churchmen, and
" terrify and provoke the Diffenters." (*w*)

What his Grace fays on the part of the pulpit,
fhall be confidered by and by.　And as for the
prefs, he reminds Mr *Walpole*, that, " moft vi-
" rulent pamphlets, publifhed daily both againft
" Church and State, gave the government no
" terror at all." (*x*)　Not fo much indeed, I dare
fay, as his Grace thought they fhould have given,
judging herein by his own feelings; no man perhaps,
of his ftation, having ever been more terrified and
difquieted by pamphlets and letters in News-pa-
pers on Church matters, than the late Dr *Secker*.
Of the fact however, or of its effects, he was far
from being fo competent a judge as Mr *Walpole*,
who was very fenfible, that it would not follow,
becaufe

(*w*) Page 20.　　(*x*) Page 21.

becaufe the miniftry were not affected by falfe and invidious charges from the prefs, refpecting their political conduct in mere ftate affairs, that they would be equally unaffected, when fo fevere a ftroke upon the religious liberties of the Colonies, as the executing the Epifcopizing fcheme would be, fhould be objected to them.

But if Mr *Walpole* faw his Grace's weaknefs in this reflection, much more would he be fcandalized when, to take off all his apprehenfions of what might happen in parliament, he found his Grace intimating, that " there feemed no neceffity that this af- " fair fhould ever come into parliament.(*y*)"

By this circumftance, the ftatesman would difcover the man and his communication, and whence he derived his principles. He would recollect too, that parliament had more than once taken a retrofpect of minifterial meafures, adopted without its fanction; and would never be more likely to do it, than when fuch meafures feemed to tend to raife feuds and animofities, difguft and difcontent, in places where the commercial interefts of *Great Britain* are fo much concerned, as in the Colonies. And if, in the progrefs of their inquiries, it fhould appear, that the Adminiftration had been preffed into this fervice by the importunity of the Bifhops in general (who have all been, according to his Grace, equally defirous of eftablifhing Epifcopacy in the Colonies, from the Revolution, to the date

of

(*y*) Page 21.

of his Letter) few would wonder, if it should be resolved, that " Episcopal power is a great griev-
." ance to this nation, and that it must rise to an
" equal height wherever Bishops are."

His Grace, however, could put Mr *Walpole* in the way of composing these stirs even in parliament. " The Administration," says his Grace, " will " easily *quiet* such of the Members as are their " friends ;" namely, by threatning to take away their places or their pensions, or by promising them to such of their friends as had them not. " The Tories must be for Bishops, if it be only to " preserve their own credit." And consequently, for Bishops invested with all the powers which tory principles ascribe as appendages to the office : for it would be impossible to keep their credit with their party, by consenting to the sending out Bishops with that limited, low-church jurisdiction, which his Grace *affects* only to desire. " And the " remainder will probably find themselves too in- " considerable to stir." *The remainder ;* that is to say, all the faithful representatives of the people, who are neither to be corrupted by the administration, nor infected by those pernicious principles of religion and government, which have been in times past so pernicious to the rights and liberties of the British subject, and so dangerous to that illustrious succession of protestant Princes, under whose Government only we can hope to enjoy them. Excellent Patriot ! excellent Archpastor of
a free

a free Proteſtant people ! who for the ſake of mag-
nifying a mere Eccleſiaſtical Office, no way eſſen-
tial to the faith or practice of Evangelical Christianity, would ſtifle the influence, on which the
preſervation of the religion and liberties of his
country chiefly depends !

It remains to conſider "the only danger,"
which, according to his Grace, "is left, *viz.* that of
"alarming or provoking the body of the Diſſen-
"ters(z)." Whom he diſtinguiſhes into, "a
"few buſy, warm men;" and ſuch as, "after ar-
"guing properly with them, have owned that they
"had little or nothing to object againſt appoint-
"ing Biſhops in Plantations of the Epiſcopal Com-
"munion(a)." And among the latter he names
Dr *Avery*, and Dr *Samuel Chandler*.

What Dr *Chandler* might ſay to Dr *Secker*, is of
little conſequence : It can hardly be ſaid, that Dr
Chandler ſpoke the ſenſe of the body of the Diſſenters, when it is ſo well known, that his connexion
with that Prelate was far from adding to his eſti-
mation among them. He is not at preſent at
hand to anſwer for himſelf. Poſſibly ſomebody
might be found, who is able to anſwer for him.
Be that as it may, I ſhall not preſume either to
accuſe him, or to apologize for him.

Dr *Avery*'s juſtification is upon a leſs precarious
footing. It is well known to ſome yet living, that
he was a principal mover of the application to the
Miniſtry,

(z) Page 22.   (a) Ibid.

Miniftry, about the time this Letter of Dr *Secker's* was written, to lay afide the project of fending Bifhops to *America*. If I am not mifinformed, he had the honour of conferring with fome of his Majefty's Minifters on the fubject, and gave them unanfwerable reafons, why a fcheme fo likely to produce difturbances in the Colonies, fhould be laid afide. What he is here reprefented to have acknowledged to the Archbifhop, is in the higheft degree improbable. He was not a man to be overawed by the folemnity, or cajoled by the affected civility of an Archbifhop. He was liberal in his fentiments, and generoufly open and unreferved in expreffing them upon all proper occafions. His conduct, in all his tranfactions, was inflexibly upright, and far exalted above all narrow, felfifh, and finifter views. No man knew all this better than the late Archbifhop *Secker*; and if this Letter is not fpurious, it is not an impoffible fuppofition, that *one* motive of its fleeping fo long in his Grace's clofet, might be, the danger of having it crofs-examined and confronted by the teftimony of fo refpectable a character.

Speaking of the oppofition to this Epifcopizing project, which might be apprehended from the body of Diffenters, his Grace delivers himfelf as follows.

" And indeed there is no modefty in faying,
" we, who are not of the Eftablifhed Church, de-
" mand as a matter of ftrict juftice, the full ex-
" ercife

" ercife of our religion here, but at the fame time
" infift that the King's epifcopal fubjects in *America,*
" with whom we have nothing at all to do, fhall
" not, even in thofe provinces where they are the
" eftablifhed Church, have the full exercife of
" theirs (*b*)."

It is pleafant enough to hear his Grace talk of *modefty,* while he is giving fuch a reprefentation as this. What would his Grace have thought of his having the full exercife of his religion, in cafe he had not been permitted to enjoy the preferments he once held in commendam, without firft receiving the communion amongft the Diffenters? It is made a part of his merit in the Biographia Britannica that he never did communicate with them, even while he appeared to belong to their Church; (*c*) whence it may eafily be conjectured, how unpalatable fuch a condition would have been to him when he was Bifhop of *Oxford.* Would not his Lordfhip have thought, that his Majefty's fubjects in *America,* while not burdened with any fuch teft, would have had a fuller exercife of their religion, than his Lordfhip, even without the ceremony of confirmation? Can a Man be faid to have the full exercife of his religion, who is excluded from the natural and equitable rights of a good fubject, unlefs he will conform to a mode of religious worfhip which he thinks to be wrong, and which fome of his brethren have thought to be even *idolatrous!*

F It

(*b*) Page 23.   (*c*) Article BUTLER (JOSEPH).

It is plain, his Grace never made this cafe of the Diffenters his own, and that he gave Mr *Walpole* only a copy of his countenance, when he told him, a little below, that, " he fhould have been a moft " hearty and zealous advocate for the Diffenters," in a cafe where they happened not to want his affif-tance, and that, " from his love of religious liber- " ty (*d*);" when he never moved a finger to relieve them in a cafe where, if he knew what religious liberty meant, he muft have known how *juftly* they think they have it not, and where an advocate of his Grace's ftation and character would have been of the greateft fervice.

There are in this fhort period, no lefs than two other mifreprefentations. For, 1. His Grace could not produce any legal authority for faying, that the Epifcopal Church of *England*, is the *eftablifhed* Church, in *any* of the American Provinces. 2. The King's Epifcopal fubjects in *America*, were not they, with whom our domeftic Diffenters, had to do in this cafe. It was their concern for, and their defire to preferve to the Americans of their own Antiepifcopal perfuafion, the *full exercife of their civil and religious rights*, (which they apprehended upon good grounds, might be encroached upon, by the admiffion of Bifhops into any of the Ame-rican Provinces) that occafioned their vigilance at the time referred to. They knew, the hardfhip of thofe legal difabilities under which they themfelves

lay

(*d*) Page 23.

lay at home. They had good reafon to believe that the influence of the eftablifhed Hierarchy contributed to continue this grievance. Their Brethren in *America* were as yet free from it, and if Bifhops were let in among them, and particularly, under the notion of prefiding in *eftablifhed* Epifcopal Churches, there was the higheft probability, they would take their precedents of Government and Difcipline from the Eftablifhment in the Mother Country, and would probably never be at reft, till they had eftablifhed it on the bafis of an exclufive Teft. They knew their American brethren thought on this fubject, juft as they themfelves did. They knew how *cautioufly* the projectors of the plan covered their march from all the Colonies, but their own confidants. They knew that, without their interpofition, the arrival of a Bifhop in *America* would probably be the firft notice the Colonifts would have of his appointment at home. They were aware of the alarm this would give them, and of the difagreeable confequences of their oppofition, with refpect to the Government. They wifely therefore, and like good patriots, fignified their apprehenfions to the Government, and ftrengthened them with fuch proofs, as entirely convinced the Miniftry, how much the public peace and welfare depended upon the fuppreffion of this pernicious project.

In this tranfaction I have good grounds to fay, that Dr *Avery* was a principal actor and advifer;

and

and would his Grace have ventured, in his life-
time, to rank the Dr among, "the *few bufy, warm*
" *men*, who only *affected* to fpeak in the name of
" the whole?" or among thofe who oppofed the
Epifcopizing fcheme through, " a wantonnefs of
" fpirit, or an oftentatious fondnefs of ufing their
" influence with great perfons, to grieve the good
" Bifhop of *Oxford* and his partizans, without
" ferving themfelves?" (*e*).

What muft their Colony-brethren have thought
of the Diffenters at home, had the latter fuffered
them to be taken by furprize, and a meafure
forced upon them, to which, if they had not loft
all memory of the firft migration of their anceftors
from *Old England*, they muft have the utmoft
averfion? What muft every difinterefted Englifh-
man have thought of them, if, poffeffed as they
were of the fenfe of the Colonies, they fhould,
out of a punctilio of complaifance to a few fuch
bufy, warm men as the B—p of O——d, have
quietly fuffered a religious war to be kindled in the
bowels of *America*, between the Non-epifcopalians
and the Members of the Church of *England*, when
they had it in their power to prevent it?

But I fhall venture to go ftill farther. Many of
the Colonifts of the Church of *England* are the
defcendants of fome of the firft fettlers, who pro-
feffed Church principles, and practifed the modes
of worfhip eftablifhed in Old *England*, in their

own

(*e*) Page 24.

own houfes, when they could not have a Minifter
to officiate among them. Yet thefe were driven
from their native land, by Epifcopal Difcipline,
merely becaufe they could not conform in *every
thing*. They left however, their principles and
practices to their pofterity, fome of whom, to this
hour, attend the Miniftry of the Epifcopal Miffionaries. But as their fathers left them likewife
memorials of their own particular fufferings from
Bifhops, they are no more in love with *American*
Epifcopacy than their anceftors were with *Englifh*
Prelacy. To fome of thefe, the idea of a Bifhop
upon the fpot, was as difgufting as to the Noncon-
formifts themfelves, and it is now well known,
that when they were folicited to join fome others
in reprefenting to the Society how much Bifhops
were wanted in the Colonies, their anfwer was,
" that they were well fatisfied with the means
" they had of worfhipping God according to the
" Liturgy, nor did they defire any thing more."

Among other uneafineffes apprehended by Mr
Walpole, as the probable effect of appointing
American Bifhops, one was, " that fuch a mea-
" fure would produce declamations in Pulpits;
" and revive the diftinction of High and Low
" among Churchmen (*f*)."

To this anxiety, his Grace adminifters the following foporific. " Now amongft the Clergy, I
" conceive it can make no difpute, for *every Man*

F 3   " of

(*f*) Page 20.

" *of character* amongſt them doth, and muſt wiſh
" it ſucceſs." His Grace ſhould have added,
" and every man amongſt them who wiſhes it
" ſucceſs, is and muſt be *a Man of character* ;"
and then the reſult muſt have been, that every one
who did not wiſh the project to ſucceed, was a re-
probate, *a Man of* no *character.*

But might not Mr *Walpole* have ſuggeſted, that
diſputes were moſt likely to be raiſed by Men of *no*
character? His Grace was free enough to confeſs,
that, " if the project were brought upon the car-
" pet, and the adminiſtration were to oppoſe it,
" ſome Clergymen (*ſome of theſe Men of character*)
" might be tempted to ſay indecent things of
" them ;" and I pray, how much leſs ſcrupulous
may we ſuppoſe Men of *no* character, who ſhould
not wiſh the project ſucceſs, would have been, in
caſe the adminiſtration had eſpouſed it? Either way
then, we ſee declamations from the pulpit, and
diſputes between Clergymen *of character*, and
Clergymen *of no character*, would have been unavoidable, had the affair come upon the carpet.
The beſt way therefore, Mr *Walpole* would think,
would be to keep it off the carpet.

But would this have ſatisfied theſe Clergymen
of character, with his Grace at their head? Let us
hear his Grace upon this queſtion. " We indeed
" do not threaten, if we are diſregarded. But they
" [the Diſſenters] have no more right to threaten
" than we : nor need they be feared if they do.
" Their

" Their threatnings have been very fafely flighted,
" in a point which they have much more at heart,
" I mean the Teft: and fo they may in this(g)."

It is, I think, pretty certain, (if we may credit
fome other parts of his Grace's Letter) that the
Clergy *of character*, particularly the Bifhops, never ceafed to defire, and we muft fuppofe, to endeavour, that Bifhops fhould be eftablifhed in *America*, from the revolution to the day of the date
of his Letter to Mr *Walpole*. During this whole
interval, thefe defires have been fo far *difregarded*,
that in his Grace's language, the affair never came
upon the carpet. If it fhould, and the adminiftration were to oppofe it, " fome of thofe Clergymen
" of character, who wifh it fuccefs, might, in his
" Grace's opinion, be tempted to fay indecent
" things of them."

Now, in my ideas, this has fomething the air
of a threat, in cafe the adminiftration fhould not
behave as thefe clergymen *of character* would have
them.

However his Grace would have it believed, that
mere *difregard*, even for fo long a time as fixty
years, had not produced the leaft murmur, that
could be called a *menace*. But where are the mor-
tals whofe patience, after fo long an interval, may
not be worn out? How far this was the cafe, with
the Bifhop of *Oxford* at leaft, in the year 1750, we
fhall fee prefently.

In

(g) Page 25.

In the mean time, it muſt be a pleaſant conſideration to Mr *Walpole*, that the prejudices of the
Jacobites and the Tories againſt the King and his
miniſtry, might be allayed by appointing Biſhops
for *America*, as his Grace ſuggeſts(*b*); adding,
that, " till theſe people are reconciled, our domeſ-
" tic affairs will never be on a firm and eaſy foot-
" ing." Indeed he gives Mr *Walpole* no great
encouragement to hope that *ſuch inſtances of kind-*
neſs, would work any great or ſpeedy reformation
among them, " but," ſays his Grace, " ſome
" good effect they muſt produce; and perſeve-
" rance in a due regimen will at length compleat
" the cure (*i*)."

Which expedient would not be unhappily hit
off, but for one objection on the part of the friends
of his Majeſty and his Government. For as this
American Epiſcopacy ſeems to have been, in his
Grace's ideas, one principal ingredient in that *due*
regimen which was to compleat the cure of Jaco-
bitiſm and Toryiſm, a *perſeverance* in the adminiſtration of it, might ſuggeſt the neceſſity of increaſing the doſe from time to time, till it ſhould
be totally modelled, not only to the taſte, but to
the conſtitution of the patients, *i. e.* till it came to
be a perfectly *Laudæan* Epiſcopacy; which would
be *an inſtance of kindneſs* to theſe prejudiced people,
to which, though it might be to his Grace's palate,

the

the friends to the Proteftant fettlement, would, no doubt, have confiderable objections.

Thus far by way of friendly *innuendo*, of what *might* happen in cafe of a refufal. In what follows, his Grace fpeaks a little plainer.

" On the other hand," fays his Grace, " I ap-
" prehend, the rejection of this propofal will do
" the Government by far more hurt amongft the
" Churchmen, than it can poffibly do them good
" amongft the Diffenters. When *the Bifhops* are
" afked about it, as they frequently are by their
" Clergy and others, what muft they anfwer?
" We cannot with truth exprefs difapprobation of
" it, or indifference to it. If we did, we fhould
" be thought unworthy of our ftations. Muft
" we then be forced to fay, that we are all fatis-
" fied of the abfolute fitnefs, the great advantages,
" the perfect fafety of the thing, and have re-
" peatedly preffed for it; but cannot prevail?
" Would not this both fadly diminifh our ability
" of ferving the Government, by fhewing how
" little credit we have with it; and make very
" undefireable impreffions on many minds, *con-*
" *cerning the King*, and thofe that are in authority
" under him; as incapable of being won by the
" arguments or intreaties of thofe, who have fo
" ftrong a zeal for them, to do *an innocent favour*
" to the Church? Still, if we cannot fucceed by
" refpectful applications, I know it is our duty to
" make the beft of the matter, and not difturb
" the

" the public welfare, becaufe, in this particular,
" we are unable to promote it. *I would fpeak as*
" *gently of the affair as ever I could, where there*
" *was danger of doing harm ; though I fpeak fo ear-*
" *neftly, where I would fain hope to do good. But*
" *no mildnefs or prudence will wholly or nearly* pre-
" vent *the abovementioned confequences* (k)."

And what are the abovementioned confequences?
Even as much hurt to Government as can arife, on
the one hand, from a diminution of the credit of
the Bifhops, and confequently of their ability of
ferving the Government ; and on the other, from
the refentment of the Clergy, on the difappoint-
ment of a project on which *all* of them, *of any
character*, have fet their hearts. And as his Grace
apprehends, that this will do the government more
hurt than any good the rejection of it will do them
among the Diffenters can make amends for, we muft
conclude that it would be at the peril of the Government to oblige the one and difoblige the other.

" We do not threaten, fays his Grace, when
" we are difregarded."—" Why no, my Lord,"
might Mr *Walpole* have anfwered, " not in the
" terms of a *Covent-Garden* bully, your Lordfhip
" only gives us *civilly* to underftand, what a neft
" of wafps your *epifcopal reprefentations* can raife
" about our ears, if we do not behave like good
" boys ; and how much lefs formidable the threat-
" nings of the Diffenters would be, than the *gentle*,
" *mild*,

(k) Page 26, 27.

" *mild*, and *prudent* remonftrances of our own
" fpiritual fathers, with a numerous clergy at
" their beck."

Did the Diffenters, when foliciting the repeal of
the Teft act, carry their menaces farther than this?
So his Grace thought fit to tell Mr *Walpole*, remind-
ing him at the fame time, that their threatnings,
on that occafion, had been very fafely flighted (*l*).

I am afraid, Mr *Walpole* would be inclined to
queftion the truth of this reprefentation; and probably, had he thought his Grace's Letter worth
his notice, would have told him, that the application of the Diffenters to have the Teft repealed,
fo far as it related to his Majefty's Proteftant fubjects, was *not* flighted. The anfwers given them
were refpectful, and they dutifully acquiefced in
the reafons that were affigned, why their requeft
could not be complied with. This is meant of
the Body of the Diffenters, which, as his Grace
has well obferved, is not to be denominated from
a few bufy, warm men among them.

It is upon record, that the wife and good King
William, was defirous to oblige the Diffenters in
this point, without any particular application from
them. It is equally well known, that the two excellent Princes, GEORGE I. and GEORGE II. were
no lefs difpofed to comply with the feveral applications made on that behalf by the Diffenters; and
fuch likewife were the fentiments of Mr *Walpole* and
his

(*l*) Page 25.

his noble brother; and such will ever be the sentiments of all true Patriots, and well wishers to the Proteſtant religion, and the Proteſtant government of this country.

There were indeed *threatnings* on thoſe occaſions, which were *not* ſlighted, *threatnings* from the high-church party, many of them, in ſubſtance, though not exactly in ſtile, the ſame with theſe *gentle* and *friendly admonitions* of the Biſhop of *Oxford*. Theſe made *due impreſſions* upon the ſtateſmen of thoſe days, whoſe experience had taught them, that it was ſafer to ſlight the threatnings of any ſort of men, rather than thoſe of an incenſed and vindictive high-church clergy. Very few, who either remember the tranſactions of thoſe times, or have read the hiſtory of them, will think, that theſe latter threatnings had a leſs ſhare in ſupporting the Teſt, than either the expediency of the law or a mere contempt for the Diſſenters.

I have now gone through his Grace's Letter to Mr *Walpole*, on the ſubject of *American* Biſhops: and the remaining queſtion is only this, Whether his Grace was capable of writing a Letter ſo full of groſs miſtakes, inconſiſtencies, artful miſrepreſentations, and unmanly calumnies, to a Stateſman, who, from the nature of his ſituation, was ſo capable of detecting and confuting them. The alternative is obvious. If the Letter is ſpurious, the *forgers* of it are unpardonable, not only on account of a baſe impoſition upon the public, but

for

for traducing the memory of a great man, who departed so lately full of days and honour, and in the odour of sanctity. If the Letter is genuine, his Encomiasts must have been egregiously mistaken, who have ascribed to him, not only eminent abilities in the province of authorship, but an uncommon measure of judgment, candour, moderation, and integrity in the administration of his high office; virtues and endowments which the writer of such a Letter must have possessed in a very moderate degree.

The whole case is now before the public: and if any one should be inclined to think that his Grace hath been treated in these papers with more freedom than is consistent with a decent regard to his Grace's station and character; let it be considered, that if this Letter is a forgery, these Remarks upon it are a full justification of his Grace from the imputations which are necessarily suggested by the contents of it. If it is genuine, be it understood, that *Truth* and *Righteousness* are no respecters of persons, are of no party, nor at all more attached to the Mitre and Lawn, than to the Sackcloth and Ashes of a pretended penitent. And be it farther noticed, that he who contrives to spread bad principles, and to recommend mischievous projects after his demise, which he does not chuse to publish and avow in his life-time, is no longer intitled to the benefit of that common maxim, *De mortuis nil nisi bonum.*

POSTSCRIPT.

POSTSCRIPT.

THAT it may not be faid that mere prejudice hath prevailed fo far in drawing up thefe
Remarks, as to leave no room for juftice; I here
declare my entire concurrence with his Grace in
one maxim adopted by him, at page 6. however
unfortunate I may think him in his application of
it to the promotion of *American* Epifcopacy.

The maxim is this. *Againft things evidently
right and ufeful, no dangers ought to be pleaded,
but fuch as are very probable and great.* His Grace
faw the *rectitude* and *ufefulnefs* of fettling Bifhops
in our American Colonies in fo ftrong a point of
light, and the *dangers* which would attend it, at
fo great a diftance, and in fo diminutive a fize,
that he ventured this aphorifm with all fecurity,
nothing doubting, but the public would readily
take his word for *one* member of his premiffes, as
a confummate Divine, and for the other, as a

Prelate

Prelate of great *moderation* and *fincerity*, which would intitle him to his conclusion of courfe.

There were however times and occafions, when and where this maxim made very little impreffion upon his Grace, and when and where the application of it, in the opinion of many ferious and thinking Chriftians, was full as appofite, as it was in the cafe of *American* Bifhops.

It is well known, that feveral very important objections have been made to fome particulars in our eftablifhed forms ; that alterations and amendments in thefe have been fuggefted by learned and confcientious men, both among the clergy and the laity ; and that they who have folicited fuch amendments, have demonftrated, to the fatisfaction of all capable and difinterefted judges, that fuch amendments would be not only *right* and *ufeful*, but *void of all danger*, except from the oppofition of thofe, who ought to be the firft to promote them.

How ftood his Grace affected to thefe alterations and amendments ? Even juft as his Grace, in this Letter, reprefents the Diffenters at home, and the Non-conforming Colonifts abroad, to be affected towards his project of epifcopizing *America*, *warm* and *bufy* and *zealous* to difappoint every thing tending to encourage them, and *threatning* the public with dolorous confequences, if any of the feveral reformations propofed, fhould take place.

For

For this purpofe his Grace's agents were fet to work in every quarter, and having once more revived the ridiculous clamour of the *danger* of the Church, they were not afhamed to reprefent the remonftrants on the behalf of a reformation, as aiming to root up the foundations of the eftablifhment; as, *feeking, under the pretence of amendment, to break loofe from all inftitutions and forms*; as propofing to *fet fire to the whole edifice, becaufe fome minute parts of it are not perfectly adapted to the reft*; and laftly, as *concurring with thofe fons of licentioufnefs, who think that laws are fuperfluous things, and that civil focieties were inftituted to be torn to pieces by difcords* (a).

Dr *Markham*, Dean of *Chrift's Church*, of whofe oratory this is a fpecimen, could hardly be unconfcious that he had here employed the figure *Hyperbole* with great freedom. But he would take it for granted his audience would underftand him, and particularly *one* of them, who had already apprifed the world how much *utility*, in cafes of this nature, had the advantage of *truth*.

It was honeft enough in him, however, to tell the company firft, and afterwards fo many of his readers as underftand Latin, where he learned his knack. For he immediately fubjoins, that, "it "was hardly poffible for him, or any one elfe to "deal in fuch matters, without calling to mind

G   "*that*

(a) See Dr Markham's *Oratiuncula*, at the end of his *Cancio ad Clerum*, before the Convocation, *Jan.* 25. 1769.

" *that man*, who among our Prelates had obtained
" the *sovereignty*, and by whose death, we grieve
" for the *diminished dignity* of our Church." A
pretty compliment, by the way, to the survivors;
to which, left he should not be understood, he adds
a little afterwards, " the Church would have a
" great loss of such a man in her most flourishing
" times, but much more in her present *penury !*"

What effect this petulant insult might have upon the venerable body to which it was addressed,
I shall not presume to guess; but I confess, when
I recollect, even without looking into the Court
calendar, ten or a dozen names who were either
actually or *virtually* present on that occasion, and
who are far from being overvalued in point of
abilities, by being put in comparison with the late
Archbishop *Secker*, my resentment is provoked,
and I am unavoidably urged to examine upon what
grounds this unjust preference is given to the Orator's Hero and grand Exemplar.

" He was, saith Dr *Markham*, a strenuous
" [*propugnator*] both of *our* faith and discipline."
OUR faith and discipline; that is, the faith and
discipline of the Church of *England*. The idea
of a Gladiator, is not quite so suitable to the character of a defender of the christian faith and discipline : and the plain meaning of this encomium
is, that his Grace was an obstinate maintainer of
whatsoever was *established*, right or wrong; whether agreeable to the Gospel of Christ, or not.
However,

However, to make his Grace look as like a good chriſtian and a good proteſtant as he could, he hath added, *ubique tamen ſine acerbitate diſſentiens*; which I know not well how to render, as, a *ſtrenuous champion* diſſenting from his adverſary *without bitterneſs*, exhibits a diſcordancy in one and the ſame character, not very eaſy to be conceived : unleſs we may be allowed to ſuppoſe that his Grace's *propugnatorial* ſpirit, was gloſſed over with an inſidious mildneſs, by way of a maſk, till he could take his adverſary at a proper advantage. For if his Grace's mildneſs and moderation, were either truly natural, or truly chriſtian diſpoſitions, it is impoſſible Dr *Markham* ſhould be put in mind of Archbiſhop *Secker*, in the midſt of the *bittereſt* railings, miſrepreſentations, and even ſcurrilities, thrown out againſt thoſe who attempted only to *reform* his Grace's beloved eſtabliſhment of faith and diſcipline.

Having done with his Grace's controverſial character, Dr *Markham* proceeds to give an account of his literary abilities, where, having allowed that, "his Grace's ſtile was not the moſt poliſhed," he inſiſts, that, "no one ever outſtripped him, "in copiouſneſs, method, and gravity."

Did the Doctor never hear of *Thomas Aquinas?* However, theſe are excellencies it muſt be owned; but excellencies of which every laborious compiler of a good common-place book may equally boaſt.

This

This *mediocrity* in his Grace's proficiency as a writer, is the more surprizing, in that we are told, at the end of the next paragraph, that, " there " never was a man of leisure who laboured more " in literary studies, than his Grace did in a most " busy station."

As Dr *Markham*, no doubt, expects to be believed, we will for once, take his word for this remarkable fact, and only inquire how his Grace acquitted himself in his department of *business*.

And here his Grace is held forth to us, as, " a " *Magistrate*, who laid it down for a principal " rule of his conduct, to be wanting to no part " of his duty, and this in the midst of a multi- " plicity of cares with which he was daily beset."

I freely acknowledge that I cannot. form an idea of a *Magistrate* in the Church of Christ, without adding to it the idea of *usurpation*. In the Church of *Antichrist*, a *Magistrate* is a necessary character. *His* representative must, from the nature of his trust, be invested with compulsive powers, equipped with an inquisition, and other means of inflicting pains and penalties upon those who dissent from his particular system.

It is not for the honour of Archbishop *Secker* to suppose that he affected *Magistracy* in the least degree ; much less, that, in the exercise of such office, he *was wanting to no part of it* ; as that must imply a desire at least to execute penal Laws

against

against Heretics and Schifmatics, to incapacitate Diffenters, by impofing upon them Tefts and Subfcriptions to points of his own devifing, and never to fuffer one of them to efcape his vigilance when he could lay hold of him.

There is, I think, but one reafon why the Archbifhop fhould defire to be invefted with the powers of *Magiftracy*. He had but poor luck in the province of *Church-champion*. He was generally worfted whenever he met his adverfary upon the plain field of Controverfy, whether he chofe to engage on Englifh ground, or went in queft of adventures to a foreign land. At home, his own artillery was dextroufly turned upon him (*b*). Abroad, his Ligurian arts and fubterfuges were completely defeated, merely by the dint of an honeft heart, a good caufe, and a fkilful hand (*c*). It is true in thefe conflicts, his Grace laid afide the *infignia* of his order, but fome how or other, the adverfary got a peep at his countenance through the chinks of his vifor, and after that, there was

G 3   no

(*b*) In a fpirited and ingenious pamphlet, intitled, *Remarks upon the Firft of three Letters againft* The Confeffional, p. 24—36. *N. B.* The *Second* and *Third* of thefe Letters are *not* the Archbifhop's, but the work of an every way inferior hand.

(*c*) See *Remarks on an anonymous Tract, intitled,* An Anfwer to Dr *Mayhew*'s Obfervations on the Charter and Conduct. of the Society for the Propagation of the Gofpel in foreign Parts. By *Jonathan Mayhew*, Paftor of the *Weftchurch* in *Bufton.* London, Reprinted for *W. Nicoll*, 1765.

no avoiding the difgrace of being vanquifhed by caitiff knights of low degree.

It is no wonder that repeated mortifications of this kind fhould raife a little afpiration in the breaft of an impatient Prelate, to an office in which he might take his amends with more advantage. How far he acted, on this confideration, in the character of a *Church-magiftrate*, Dr MARK-HAM may know better than I do. But whatever his Grace's diligence and vigilance were in this department, it is plain, if we may believe Dr *Markham*, he had very little fuccefs; for the Dr tells us, not without fome feeming regret, that, " there never was a time when men lived and " thought more according to their own judg-" ment." Whereas, if things had proceeded profperoufly on the *Magiftratical* plan of faith and difcipline, men ought to have lived and thought according to the judgment of Archbifhop *Secker* and Dr *Markham*.

The Doctor concludes his panegyric (which he modeftly acknowledges to be *fhort* and *jejune*) with the following flourifh of his art. " In fome men " we difcern an excellent genius, and a multipli-" city of fcience, in others, prudence, authority, " probity, conftancy; but we fhall not eafily find " one in whom all thefe have fo abundantly met " together."

I have no inclination to diffect this complication of excellencies; let every one judge of it as he

fees

fees caufe. I allow, on the one hand, that an exalted ftation is a great *brightener*, and on the other,
that an *Oxford* Orator may be indulged in a little
fiction; but his Grace's writings are *ferious* things,
and are a juft *criterion* for any one who is difpofed
to verify this accumulation of virtues and good
qualities, without looking for a parallel either a-
mong the living or the dead.

It is as impoffible for me to mention an *Oxford*
Orator without thinking of Dr *Burton* *d*), as it was
for Dr *Markham* to fcourge the advocates for reformation, without thinking of Archbifhop *Secker*.

Dr *Burton* takes his Grace up indeed a little late
in life, not fooner than his 28th year; whence our
great grandchildren, reading the contents of this
panegyric in its *fortieth* edition, will naturally conclude, that his Grace owed his immenfe proficiency
in *omni fcibili* (Phyfick excepted) folely to the doctrine and difcipline of the univerfity of *Oxford*; little dreaming that he received the flighteft rudiments
among the " *irritable, perverfe, malignant, fediti-*
" *ous*, and *intolerably tyrannical* Puritans(*e*)." And
yet, as he turned out in the end, fo *compleatly furnifhed with imperatorial arts* (*f*), it is not at all un-
natural to fuppofe that he might have picked up

G 4   and

(*d*) Johannis Burton ad amicum Epiftola; five commen-
tariolus Thomæ Secker, Archiep. Cantuar. Memoriæ Sacer.
Oxonii, e Typographeo Clarendoniano. 1768.

(*e*) Epift. p. 27, 28.   (*f*) Page 14.

and retained some flight maxims of Hierarchical discipline among these *tyrannical* Dissenters, with whom his early connexions are not yet absolutely . forgotten.

I am sorry my time will not allow me to go through this elaborate Epistle, which furnishes in every page abundant matter for very edifying reflections, particularly on the frailty of bigoted and injudicious panegyrists, who, void of every idea of justice, moderation, or propriety, where their idol is to be exhibited, give occasion to those who are not quite so prone to credulity, to look farther into a character so bedaubed with fulsome adulation, than they might otherwise be disposed to do.

Dr *Burton*, for example, holds up his Grace as one of the *princes of Critics* in Hebrew literature, and for this he sends us to Mr *Merrick*'s Annotation on the Psalms (*g*). This might pass well enough with those who took Dr *Burton* for a competent judge, at least for two or three months after the publication of his Epistle. But Dr *Gregory Sharpe*, having, after that interval, shewn how far his Grace had waded out of his depth in that province, the encomium now serves for nothing, but to give suspicions, that there are more of them in the pamphlet, upon equally precarious grounds.

(*g*) Epist. page 6.

grounds (*b*). Add to this, that some suspicions
having been raised by the freedom of his Grace's
speculations on revealed religion in the earlier part
of his life, nothing could be more injudicious
than to attempt to embellish his Grace's character,
by sending the reader to a few insipid cavils
against some striking parts of a very learned and
able *Defence of CHRISTIANITY* (*i*).

Again, it was objected to his Grace, that he
was out of measure provoked at every attempt to
amend or reform our Ecclesiastical system in those
particulars where it is most exceptionable : that
whenever such proposals appeared, he was out of
all patience, summoning his Myrmidons from
every quarter, and oftentimes lending his own
hand to the confutation of these *Innovators* and
Schismatics. This, numbers of his Grace's admirers would never believe, supposing that his
Grace, who had profited so much by his own
free examination, could not be so violently embit-
tered himself, or afford his patronage and countenance to those who were, against men who had an
equal right to judge for themselves. But Dr
Burton soon put the matter out of doubt, by acknowledging

(*b*) *Vid.* A Letter to the Right Reverend the Lord Bishop
of *Oxford*, from the Master of the *Temple*, containing some
Strictures made by his Grace the late Archbishop of *Canterbury*,
in the Reverend Mr *Merrick*'s Annotations on the Psalms.
London, 1769.

(*i*) See the *Remarks* cited above, Note (*b*) p. 87.

knowledging in one place, his Grace for the author of the feeble *Anfwer* to Dr *Mayhew* (*k*), and, in another, by divulging, that his Grace not only undertook the office of *propugnator* himfelf, againft the *flanders* of *Schifmatics* and *Innovators*, but ufed the *vicarious* affiftance of others who fought under his ftandard (*l*).

It is true, the Dr fays, he took the fame courfe with the calumnies of the papifts. It might be fo; but the evidence *here* is a little obfcure: in the other cafe it is clear and decifive.

It has been often afferted, and as often denied, that his Grace kept a record of clerical delinquents, commonly called a *black book*, in which were regiftred the names and offences of thofe who had the misfortune to fall under his Grace's difpleafure; and that the better to detect defaulters, his Grace had his fpies and emiffaries properly diftributed to give the neceffary information —Dr *Burton* feems to give credit to the affirmative, by affuring us, that his Grace, " animadverted upon every thing relat-
" ing to the Clergy; that he had his *internuntii*,
" and ufed the miniftry of others in his difquifi-
" tions; fought out and noted every thing; and
" finally, *digefted his difcoveries into a kind of Fafti*,
" by way of a provincial hiftory, for the ufe of his
" fucceffors (*m*)." It would be ftrange if there
fhould

(*k*) Epift. page 28.   (*l*) Ibid. p. 21.
(*m*) Page 25.

should not be one column of this calendar appropriated to the *carbone notandi*.

But our greatest obligations to Dr *Burton* arise from his candid and undisguised account of the motives of his Grace's zeal for *American* Episcopacy. His Grace, it seems, understood by his books, that Episcopal government was of apostolical original : He perceived likewise [how, it is not said, perhaps by *instinct*] that there was a kindred connexion between *Episcopacy* and *Monarchy*. (*n*) And with these convictions upon his mind, " what wonder, saith Dr *Burton*, that our Arch-
" prelate should favour the pious desires of those
" Americans, who having embraced the faith
" and discipline of the Church of *England*, covet-
" ed to have episcopal administrations more with-
" in their reach ?" This was kind and compassionate!

But the misfortune is, that the posthumous publication of his Grace's Letter to Mr *Walpole*, hath made it questionable, whether these motives did not work considerably towards their effect, *without* these *pious desires*, and long before his Grace was possessed of the Archprelacy. That Dr *Burton* was well acquainted with his Grace's *motives* for promoting Episcopal government in *America*, there can be no doubt, after his commerce of friendship with his Grace, for more than forty years(*o*). But some possibly may suspect, that
the

(*n*) Page 26.   (*o*) Page 4.

the Dr knew little more of their *operation* than merely the *oftenfible* parts of it.

And yet from his affigning, or at leaft intimating a *third* motive for his Grace's zeal in this American bufinefs, I am apt to think Dr *Burton* knew more of this matter than he thought fit to divulge.

It feems our domeftic Diffenters, forming their judgment upon Dr *Secker*'s gentlenefs and lenity, and his earneftnefs to fupport the right of toleration (not without fome retrofpect, it is likely, to his more early principles and connexions) expected his Grace would at a proper time, " betray to " them the privileges and authority of the Church " of *England*(*p*)."

There was no way fo effectual to convince them of their miftake, as to difcover his ardent zeal to epifcopize their brethren in *America*. What other methods his Grace might take to undeceive them, it is not material to inquire. According to Dr *Burton*, it muft have been this circumftance in his Grace's conduct which chiefly opened their eyes, as it derived upon his Grace their moft furious refentment.

This being the cafe, we have here a *third* motive for his Grace's zeal for *American* Epifcopacy, diftinct from *Apoftolical* and *Monarchical* relations, inducing a fufpicion, that the *impious averfion* of *fome* to *American* Epifcopacy, might have as great a fhare

(*p*) Page 27.

a share in his Grace's attempts to establish it, as the *pious desires* of *others*.

If it were worth the while, one might pick out abundant matter of amusement, from a comparison of Dr*Burton*'s Elogy with that of Dr*Markham*'s. Both of them seem to have been conscious, that the transmitting the most unexceptionable characters to posterity, without some alloy of human infirmity, hath given occasion to the inquisitive reader oftentimes to question the good faith of the historian, or the sincerity of the panegyrist. They seem however not to be agreed, where the *nævi* in Archbishop *Secker*'s portrait should be inserted.

Dr *Markham* is inclined to place the chief imperfection in his Grace's stile. But this Dr *Burton* cannot be supposed to allow; having submitted his own valuable labours to his Grace's polishing hand, which, according to the Dr, performed this office with the utmost accuracy (*q*).

Dr *Markham*, again, thinks, that, "the chief duty of *Magistracy*, is to apply, " with diligence " to the ordering those businesses which occur in " the daily course of things;" and in this article, the Dr affirms, that the Archbishop, " in the " multiplicity of cares with which he was dis- " tracted, neglected nothing."

But Dr *Burton* is of another opinion; he *requires* in a Magistrate *an imperious obstinacy and arrogance*, in which, according to him, his Grace was extremely

(*q*) Epist. page 30.

tremely defective ; and informs us, that, had his
Grace exercifed his authority to the full, and not
given_way to the times, he would have much more
effectually provided for the common good. " For
" had this *Prince of Ecclefiaftics* exerted himfelf,
" he might, according to Dr *Burton*, (in con-
" junction with his Majefty, both of them acting
" as the avengers and fatellites of defpifed and
" violated Religion) have totally defeated that
" hundred-headed beaft, *Impiety*, which paraded
" with impunity among almoft all ranks of men."
And he gives us no obfcure intimations, that had
he been in his Grace's feat, matters would have
gone much better ; that is to fay, " Authority
" would have been reftored to the Laws, its pro-
" per honour to piety, reverence to the Ecclefiaf-
" tical order, *nor, perhaps, would the* Americans
" *have been deprived of an Hierarchy* (r)." Such
is the courage and fpirit of thofe who breathe *the
atmofphere of wholefome feverities !*

This *lenity* it is, that Dr *Burton* exhibits as the
late Archbifhop's grand foible ; taking care however to inform us, that, " it was not fo much the
" effect of the *fentiments* or the *will* of the man,
" as of a certain *political neceffity* of the times (s)."
In which, I am apt to believe, few people who
knew his Grace, will difagree with him.

Such are the encomiums of the Doctors, *Burton* and *Markham*, who, by their officious interpofition,

(r) Epift. page 35, 36.   (s) Page 36.

polition, may be fairly faid to have left their Hero in a much worfe condition than they found him, and (to borrow an expreffion from the celebrated *Junius*) " to have injured him by their affiftance."

On this charge of *lenity*, however, I am of opinion, a willing advocate might find fomething to fay for his Grace. There certainly were times and occafions when he was by no means defeсtive in this *arrogance of Magiftracy* required by Dr *Burton.* And I will only add, that it would be to his Grace's honour, if it could be proved, that, in thofe inftances, he was lefs influenced by his own temper and principles, than by the counfels and inftigation of fuch men as thefe adulatory Orators.

Г I N I S.